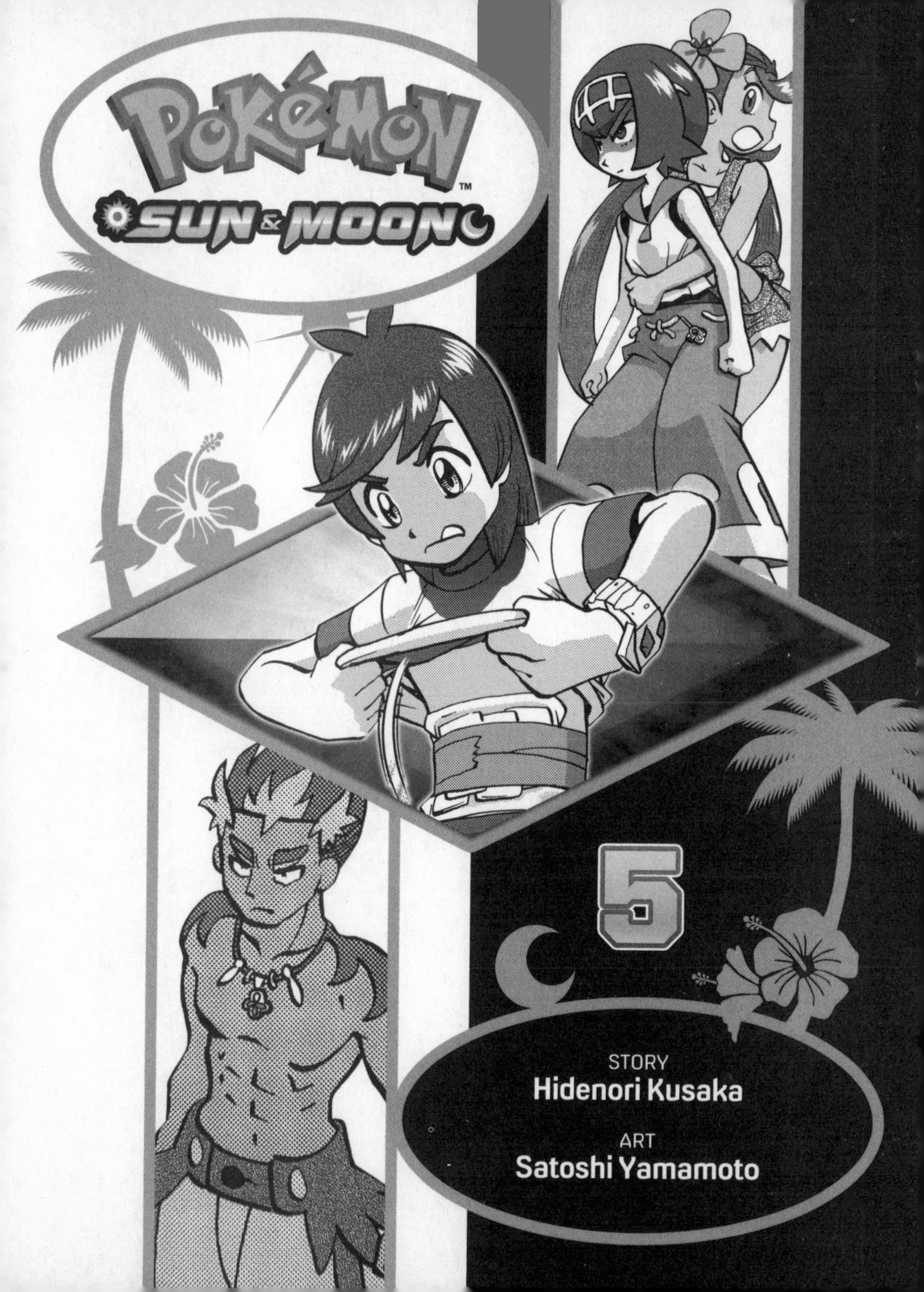
POKÉMON™
SUN & MOON
5
STORY
Hidenori Kusaka
ART
Satoshi Yamamoto

Introduction

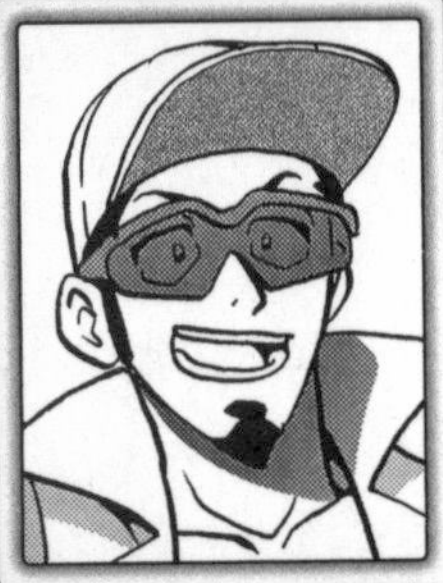

Professor Kukui

A Pokémon researcher with a laboratory on Melemele Island. An expert on Pokémon moves who likes to experience these Pokémon moves used against himself!

Moon

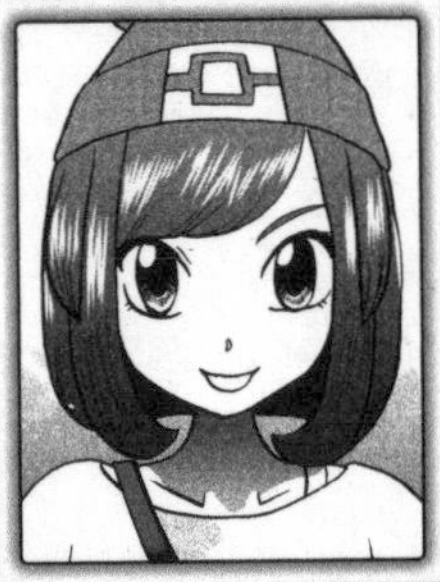

Another of the main characters in this tale. A pharmacist who has traveled to Alola from a faraway region. She is a self-confident, original thinker. She is also an excellent archer.

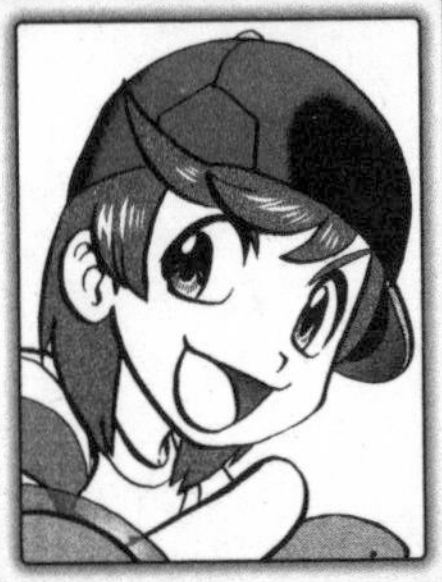

Sun

One of the main characters in this tale. A young Pokémon Trainer who makes a living doing all sorts of odd jobs, including working as a delivery boy. His dream is to save up a million dollars!

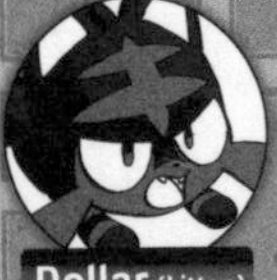

Dollar (Litten)

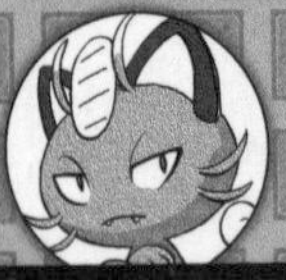

Cent (Alolan Meowth)

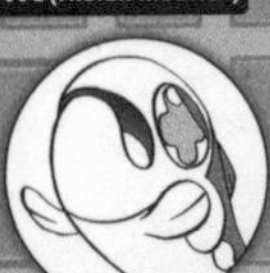

Quarter (Wishiwashi)

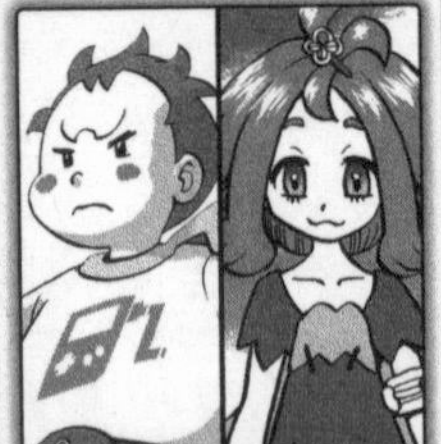

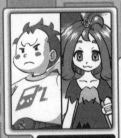

Acerola/ Sophocles

Skilled Trainers and the trial captains of Ula'ula Island.

Kiawe, Mallow, Lana

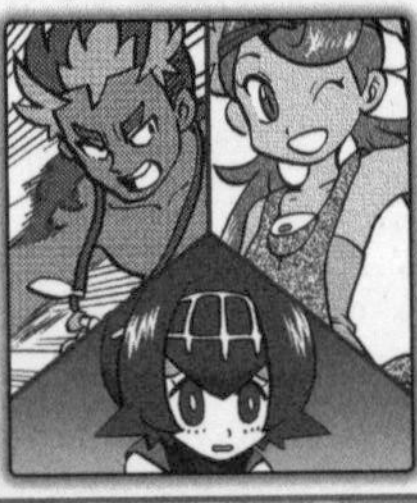

Skilled Trainers and the trial captains of Akala Island.

Character

Guzma

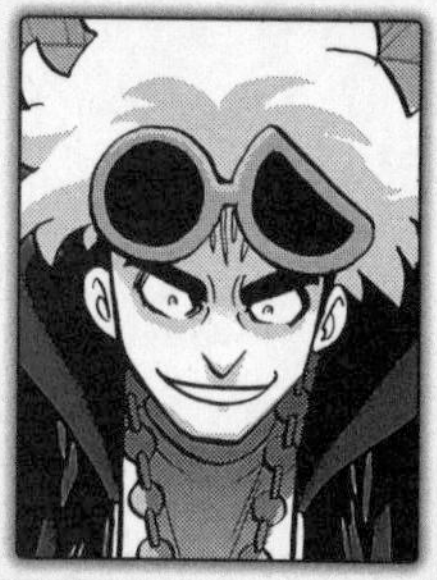

The leader of Team Skull, an evil organization that is causing trouble all over the Alola region.

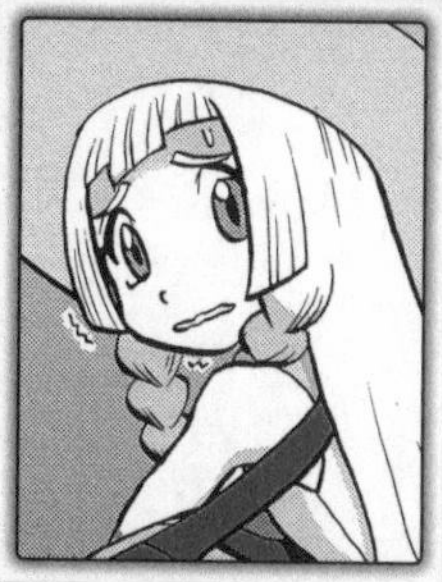

Lillie

A timid girl found washed up on the beach. She carries a strange Pokémon whom she calls Nebby.

Gladion

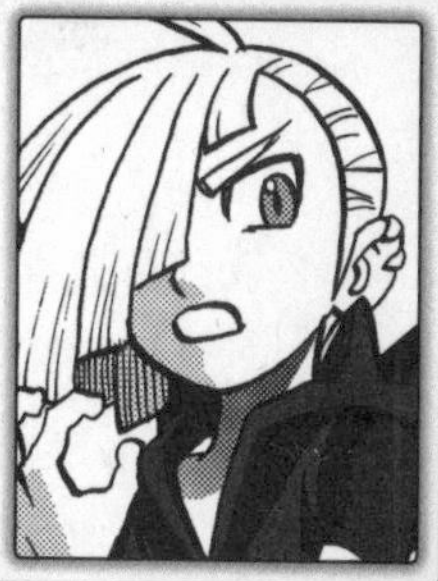

A loner with a mysterious Pokémon named Type: Null. Why is he so interested in a mysterious rift in the sky...?

The Story Thus Far...

The Alola region consists of numerous tropical islands. Moon, a pharmacist from another region, comes to this flower-filled vacation paradise on an important errand. On one of Alola's pristine beaches, she meets a boy named Sun. Sun works various odd jobs in addition to the delivery service he runs in order to reach his goal of saving up a million dollars. Moon doesn't understand why he would want so much money, but they become friends and travel to Professor Kukui's laboratory together. Meanwhile, at Iki Town on Melemele Island, preparations are in full swing for the Full Power Festival...

Each of the four islands of Alola have an Island Guardian called a Tapu. Recently, the Tapu have become agitated... The island leaders use the festival's Pokémon tournament to choose a champion to get to the root of the problem and soothe the Tapu. So when Sun defeats Gladion in the final match, he is sent off on the Island Challenge with Moon. On Akala Island, Moon witnesses a battle between Tapu Lele and a mysterious being who appears through a rift in the sky. Sun wins the respect of the Alola trial captains in battle and then fights Gladion again—this time for real—at the Ruins of Life. Sun defeats him by using the Z-Move that Kiawe taught him and then offers a special berry to Tapu Lele...

CONTENTS

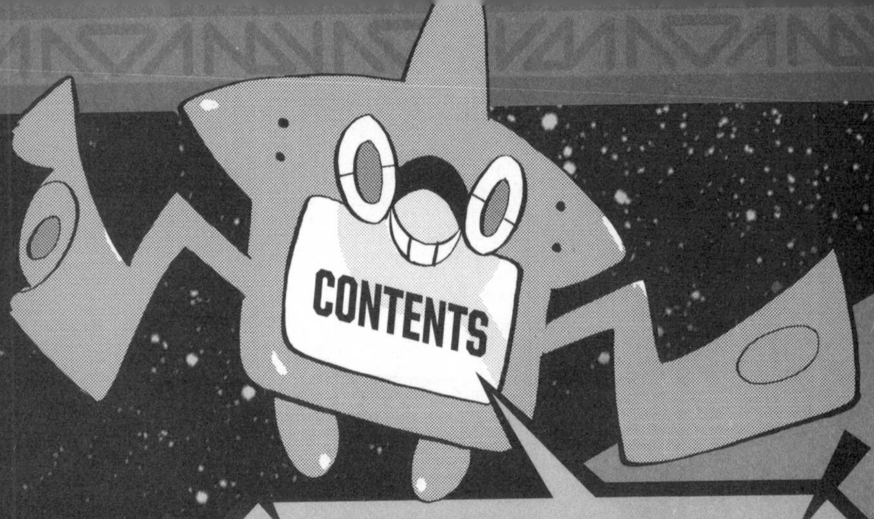

Zzt zzt... ♫

Adventure 14
Flash and Cosmog's Secret

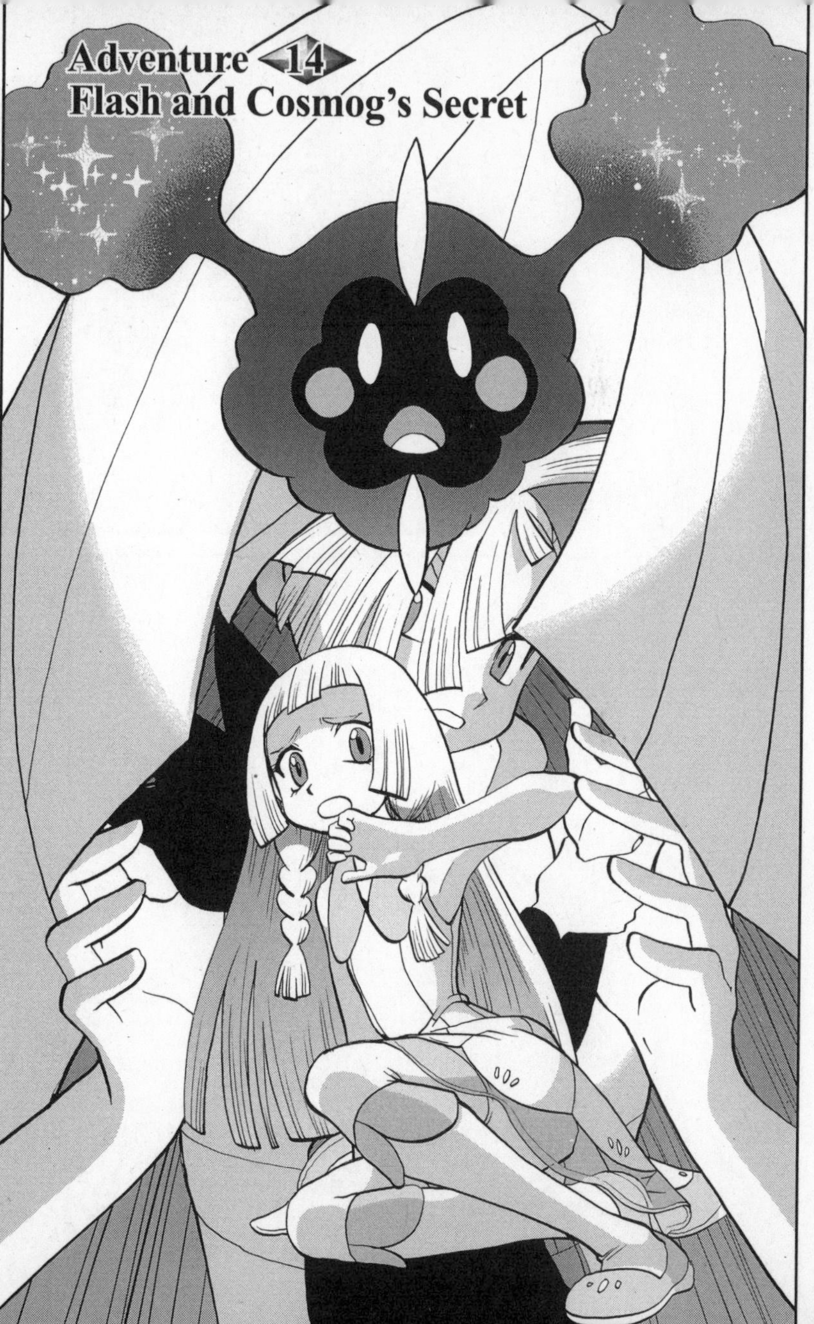

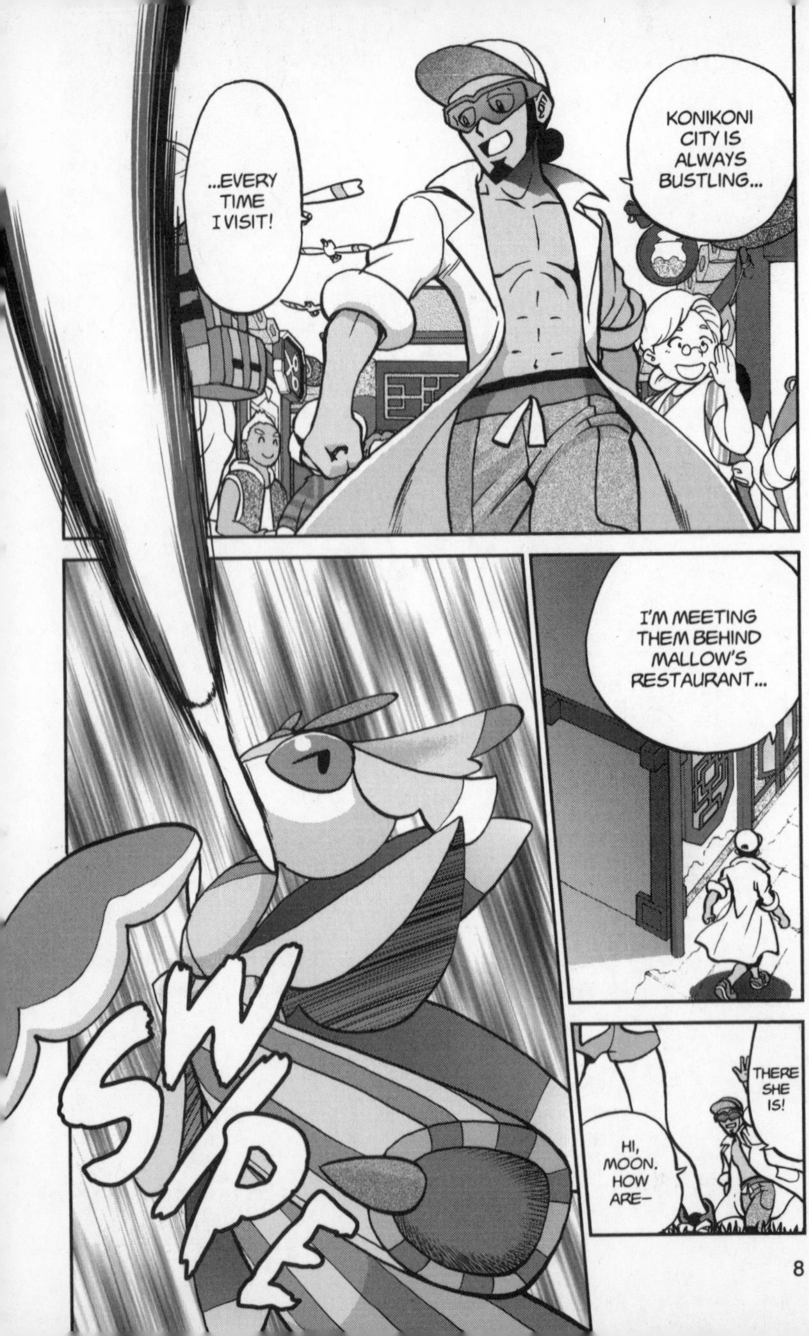
KONIKONI CITY IS ALWAYS BUSTLING...
...EVERY TIME I VISIT!
I'M MEETING THEM BEHIND MALLOW'S RESTAURANT...
THERE SHE IS!
HI, MOON. HOW ARE—
SWIPE

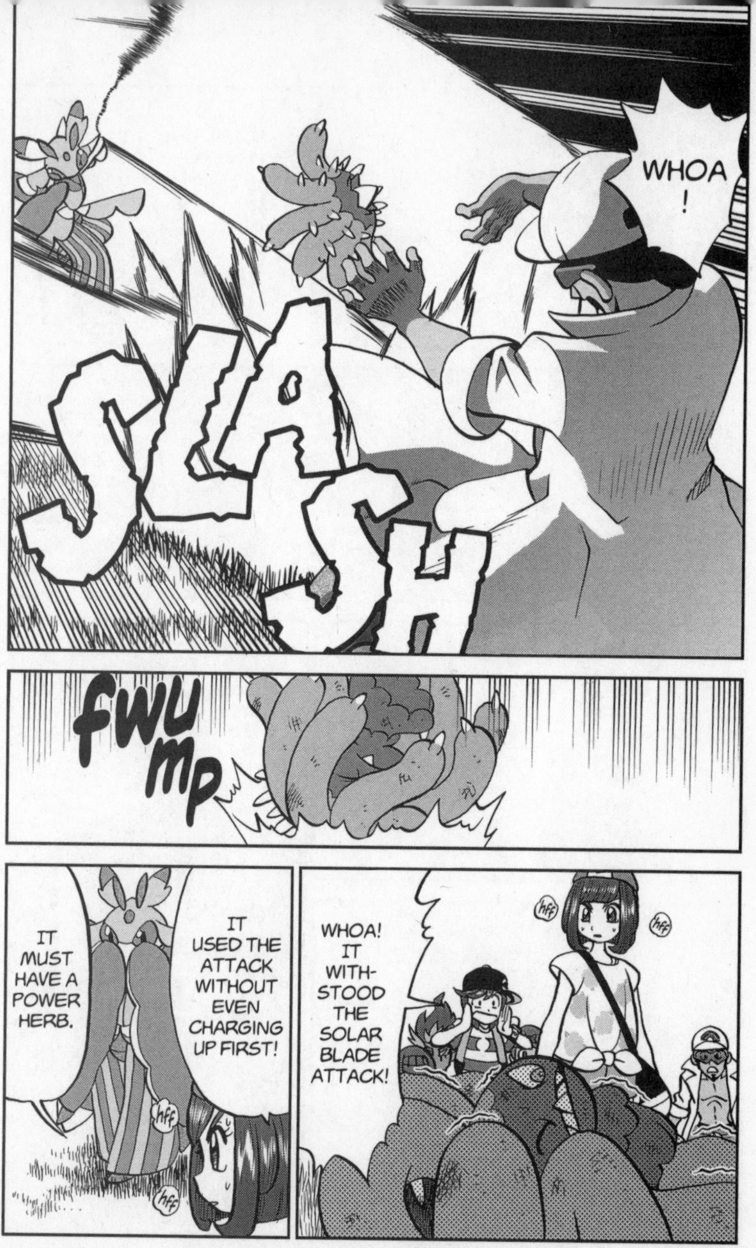
WHOA!
SLASH
fwump
WHOA! IT WITHSTOOD THE SOLAR BLADE ATTACK!
hff
hff
IT USED THE ATTACK WITHOUT EVEN CHARGING UP FIRST!
IT MUST HAVE A POWER HERB.
hff
hff

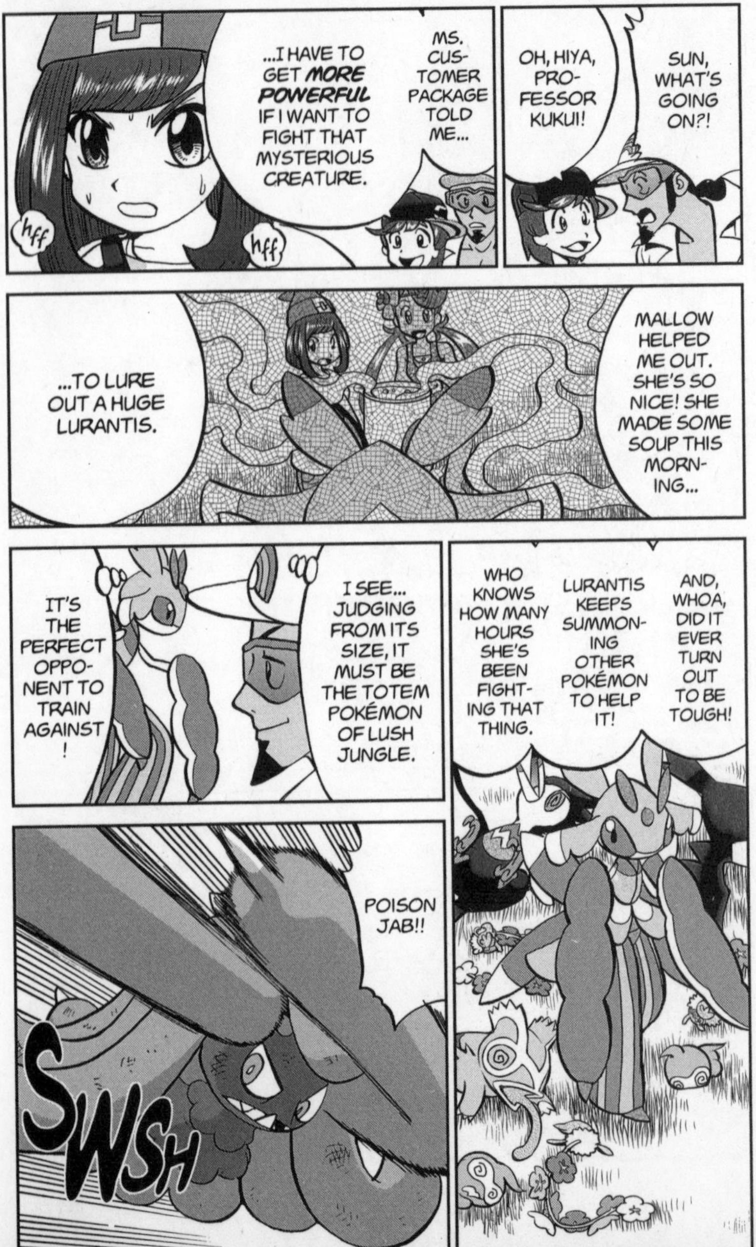
SUN, WHAT'S GOING ON?!
OH, HIYA, PROFESSOR KUKUI!
MS. CUSTOMER PACKAGE TOLD ME...
...I HAVE TO GET **MORE POWERFUL** IF I WANT TO FIGHT THAT MYSTERIOUS CREATURE.
hff
hff
MALLOW HELPED ME OUT. SHE'S SO NICE! SHE MADE SOME SOUP THIS MORNING...
...TO LURE OUT A HUGE LURANTIS.
AND, WHOA, DID IT EVER TURN OUT TO BE TOUGH!
LURANTIS KEEPS SUMMONING OTHER POKÉMON TO HELP IT!
WHO KNOWS HOW MANY HOURS SHE'S BEEN FIGHTING THAT THING.
I SEE... JUDGING FROM ITS SIZE, IT MUST BE THE TOTEM POKÉMON OF LUSH JUNGLE.
IT'S THE PERFECT OPPONENT TO TRAIN AGAINST!
POISON JAB!!
SWSH

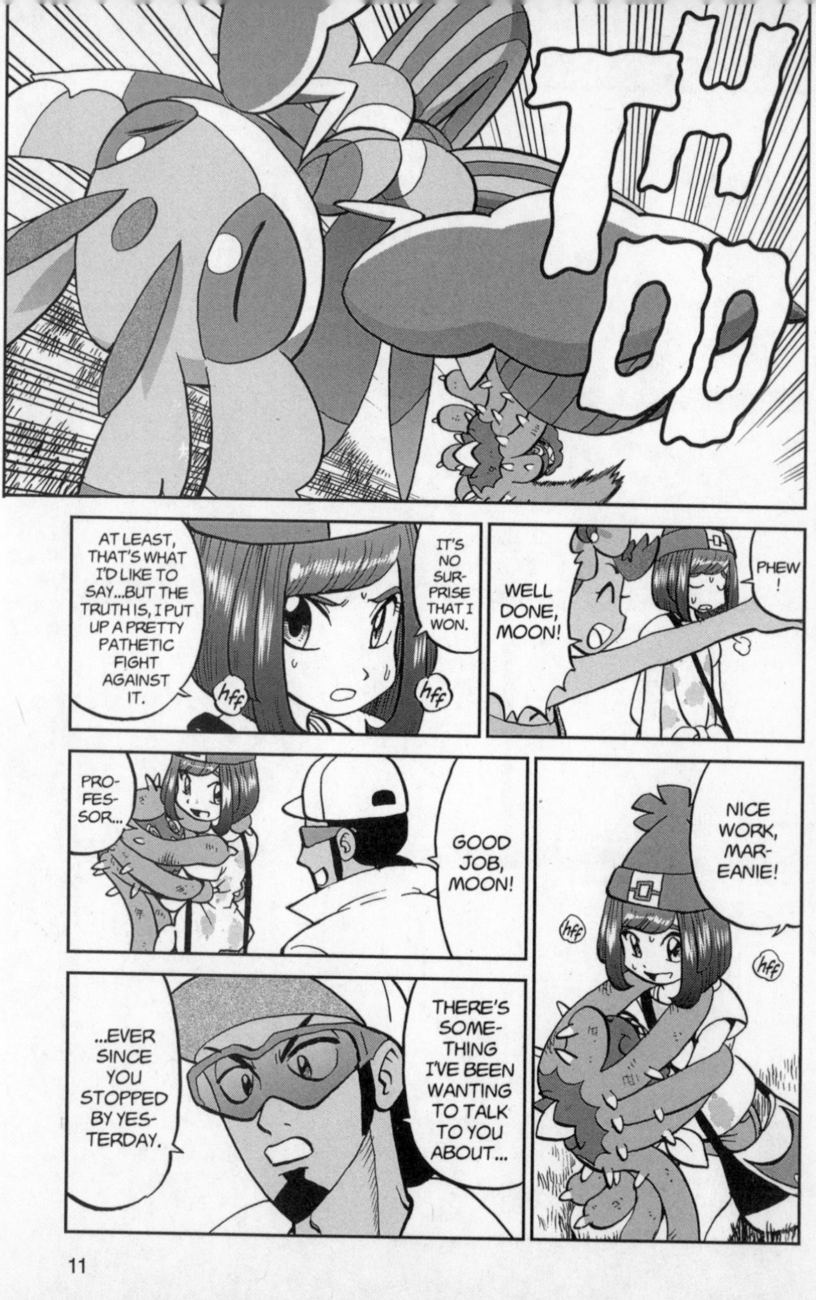
THOOD
WELL DONE, MOON!
PHEW!
IT'S NO SURPRISE THAT I WON.
hff
hff
AT LEAST, THAT'S WHAT I'D LIKE TO SAY...BUT THE TRUTH IS, I PUT UP A PRETTY PATHETIC FIGHT AGAINST IT.
NICE WORK, MAREANIE!
hff
hff
GOOD JOB, MOON!
PROFESSOR...
THERE'S SOMETHING I'VE BEEN WANTING TO TALK TO YOU ABOUT...
...EVER SINCE YOU STOPPED BY YESTERDAY.

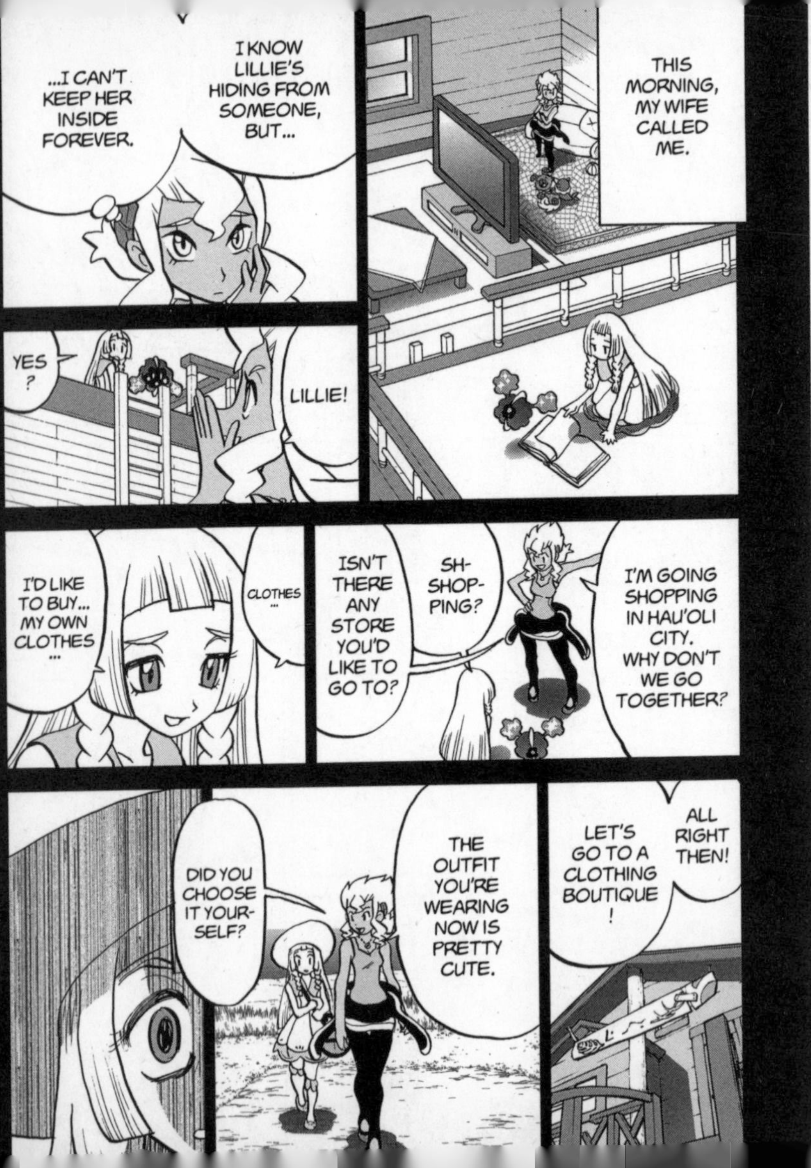
THIS MORNING, MY WIFE CALLED ME.
I KNOW LILLIE'S HIDING FROM SOMEONE, BUT...
...I CAN'T KEEP HER INSIDE FOREVER.
LILLIE!
YES?
I'M GOING SHOPPING IN HAU'OLI CITY. WHY DON'T WE GO TOGETHER?
SH-SHOPPING?
ISN'T THERE ANY STORE YOU'D LIKE TO GO TO?
CLOTHES...
I'D LIKE TO BUY... MY OWN CLOTHES...
ALL RIGHT THEN!
LET'S GO TO A CLOTHING BOUTIQUE!
THE OUTFIT YOU'RE WEARING NOW IS PRETTY CUTE.
DID YOU CHOOSE IT YOURSELF?

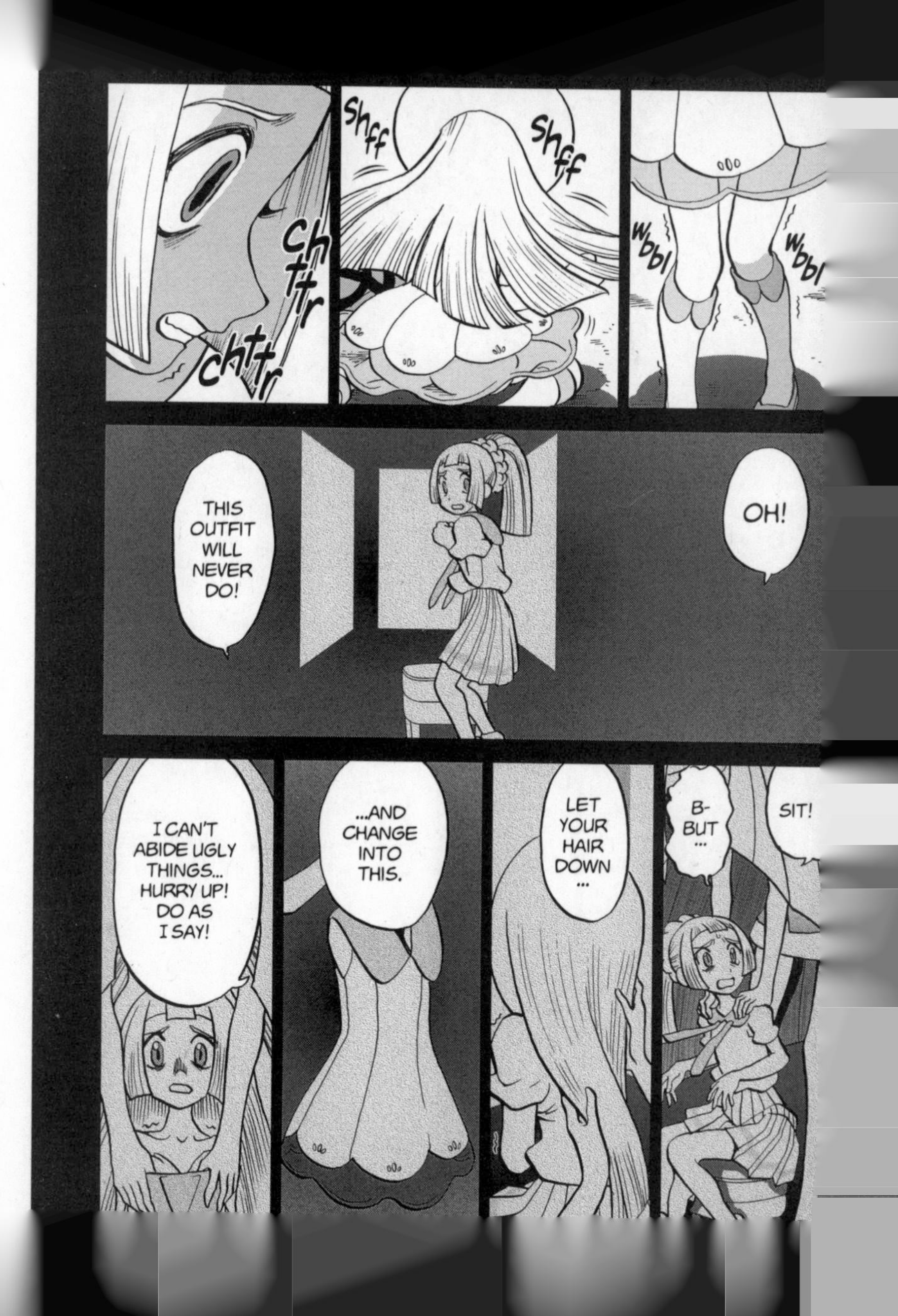
wbbl
wbbl
shff
shff
chttr
chttr
OH!
THIS OUTFIT WILL NEVER DO!
SIT!
B-BUT...
LET YOUR HAIR DOWN...
...AND CHANGE INTO THIS.
I CAN'T ABIDE UGLY THINGS... HURRY UP! DO AS I SAY!

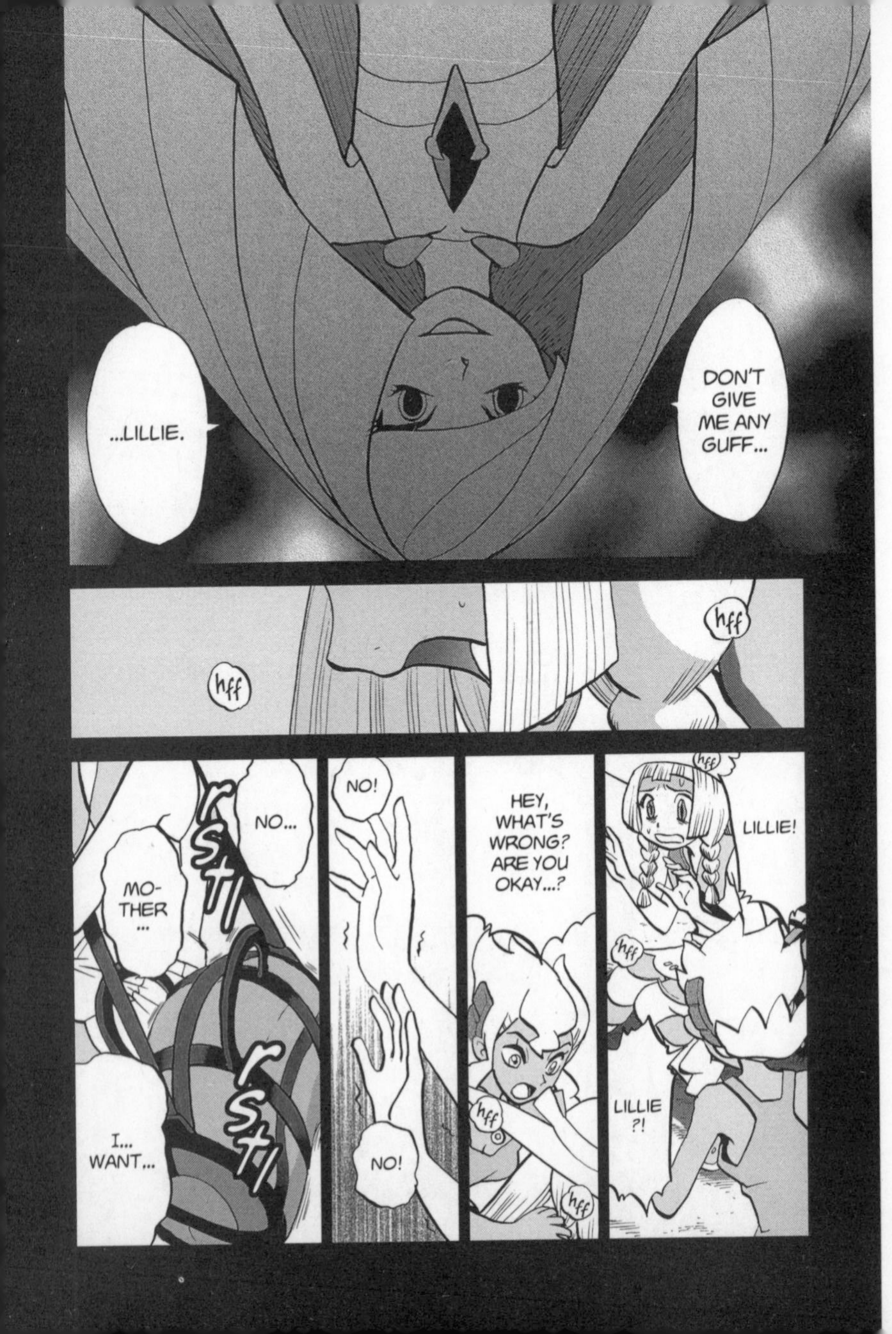
DON'T GIVE ME ANY GUFF...
...LILLIE.
hff
hff
hff
LILLIE!
hff
LILLIE ?!
HEY, WHAT'S WRONG? ARE YOU OKAY...?
hff
hff
NO!
NO!
NO...
MO-THER ...
rstl
rstl
I... WANT...

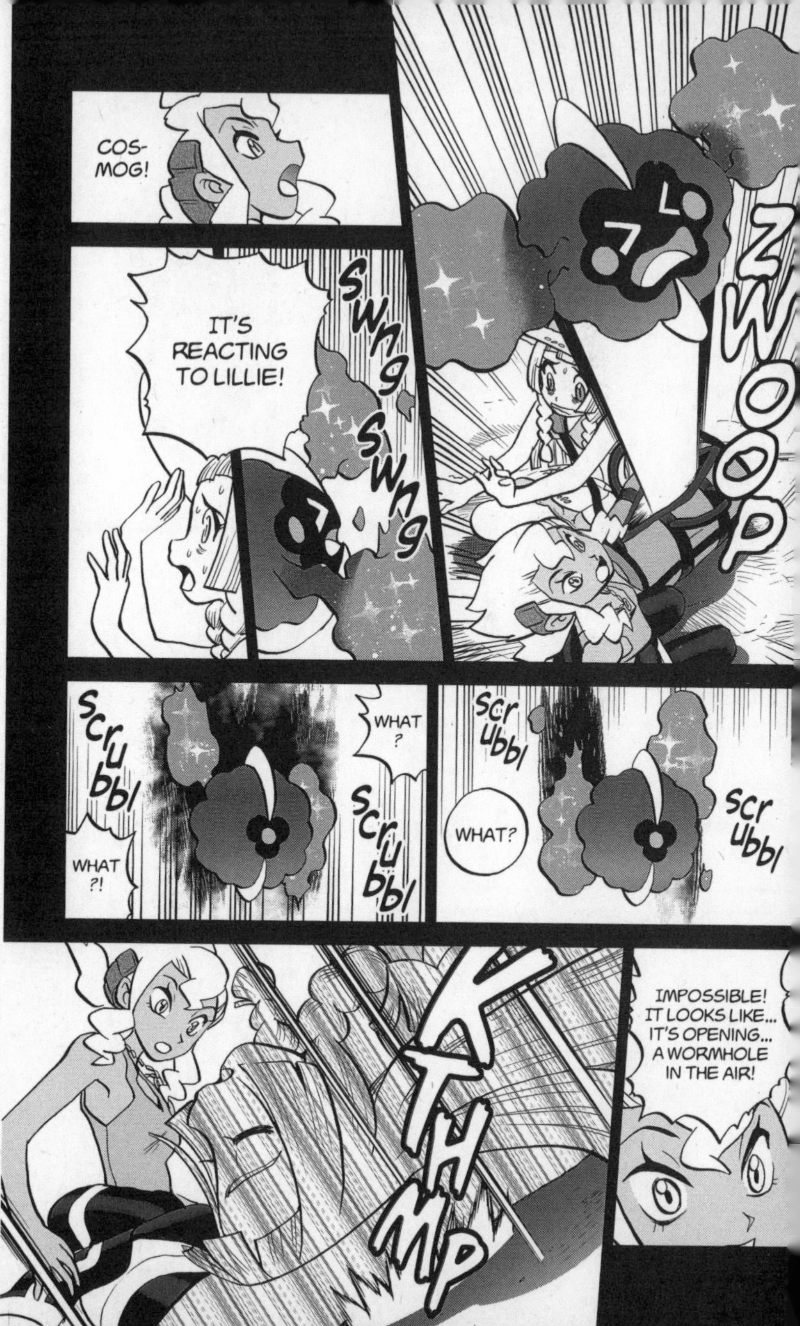
ZWOOOOP
COS-MOG!
IT'S REACTING TO LILLIE!
swng swng swng
scr ubbl
WHAT?
scr ubbl
WHAT ?
scrubbl
scrubbl
WHAT ?!
IMPOSSIBLE! IT LOOKS LIKE... IT'S OPENING... A WORMHOLE IN THE AIR!
THUMP

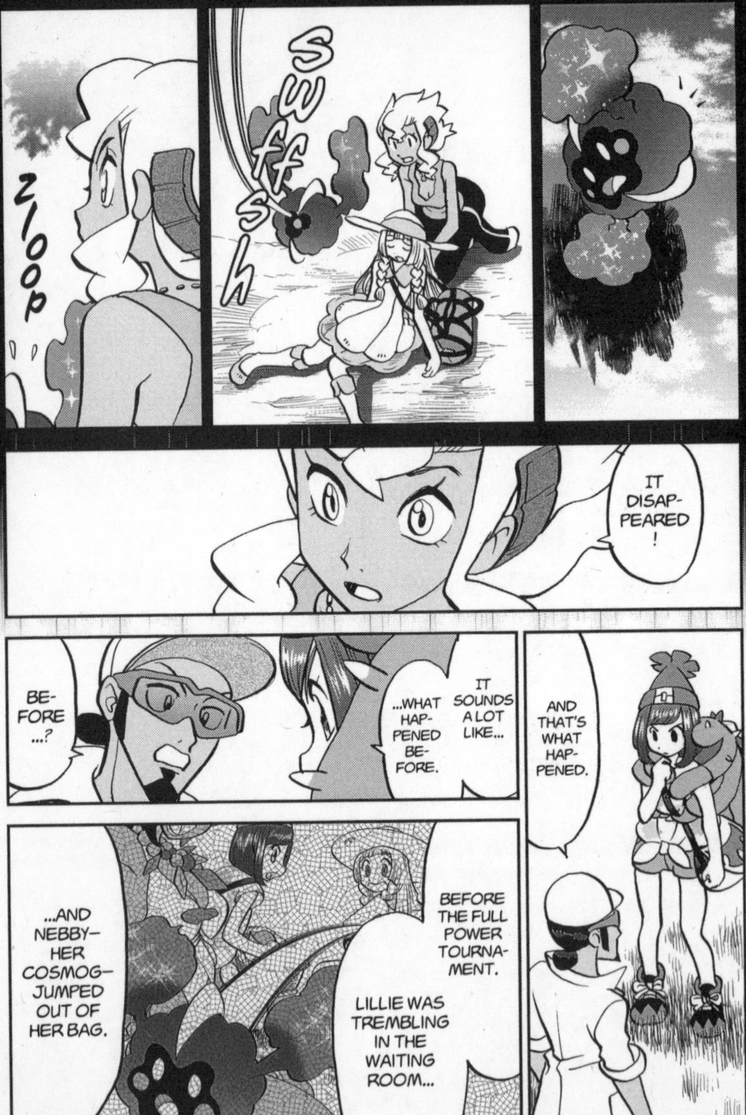
SWFFSH
ZLOOP
IT DISAPPEARED!
AND THAT'S WHAT HAPPENED.
IT SOUNDS A LOT LIKE...
...WHAT HAPPENED BEFORE.
BEFORE...?
BEFORE THE FULL POWER TOURNAMENT.
LILLIE WAS TREMBLING IN THE WAITING ROOM...
...AND NEBBY—HER COSMOG—JUMPED OUT OF HER BAG.

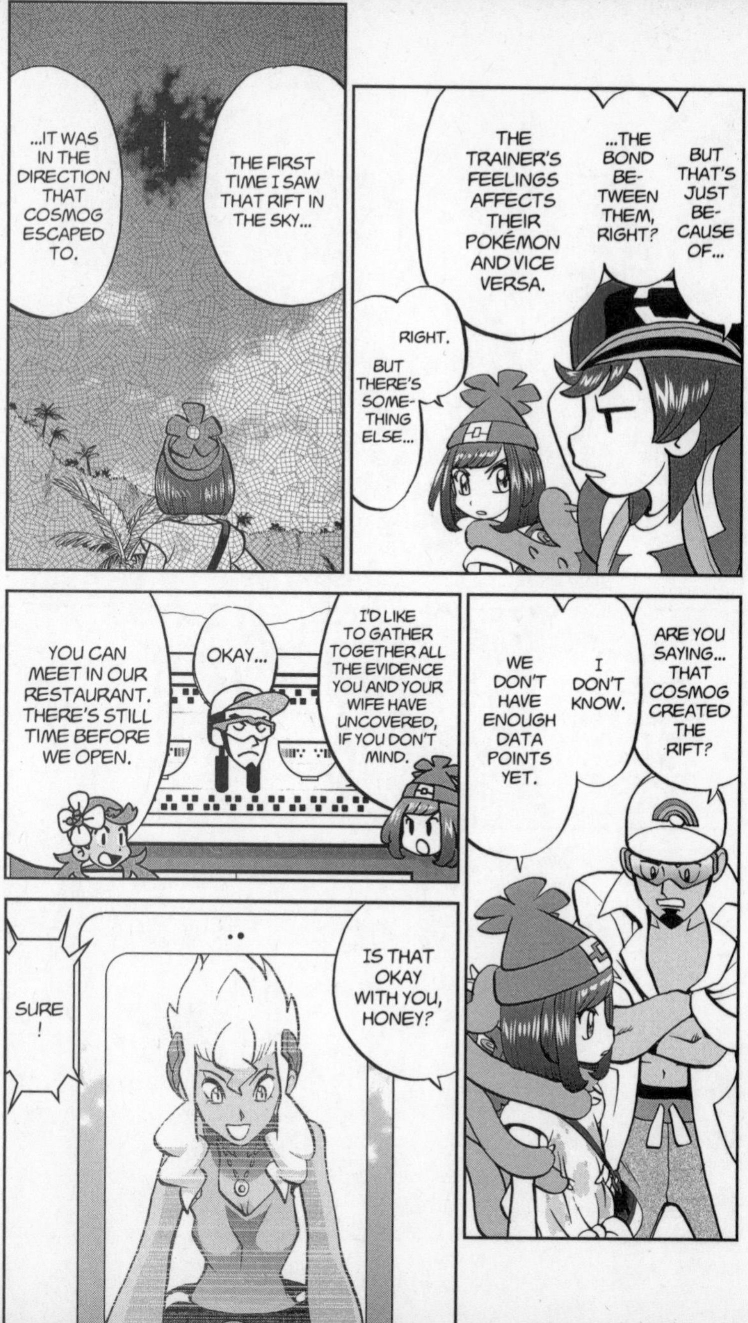
BUT THAT'S JUST BE-CAUSE OF...
...THE BOND BE-TWEEN THEM, RIGHT?
THE TRAINER'S FEELINGS AFFECTS THEIR POKÉMON AND VICE VERSA.
RIGHT. BUT THERE'S SOME-THING ELSE...
THE FIRST TIME I SAW THAT RIFT IN THE SKY...
...IT WAS IN THE DIRECTION THAT COSMOG ESCAPED TO.
ARE YOU SAYING... THAT COSMOG CREATED THE RIFT?
I DON'T KNOW.
WE DON'T HAVE ENOUGH DATA POINTS YET.
I'D LIKE TO GATHER TOGETHER ALL THE EVIDENCE YOU AND YOUR WIFE HAVE UNCOVERED, IF YOU DON'T MIND.
OKAY...
YOU CAN MEET IN OUR RESTAURANT. THERE'S STILL TIME BEFORE WE OPEN.
IS THAT OKAY WITH YOU, HONEY?
..
SURE!

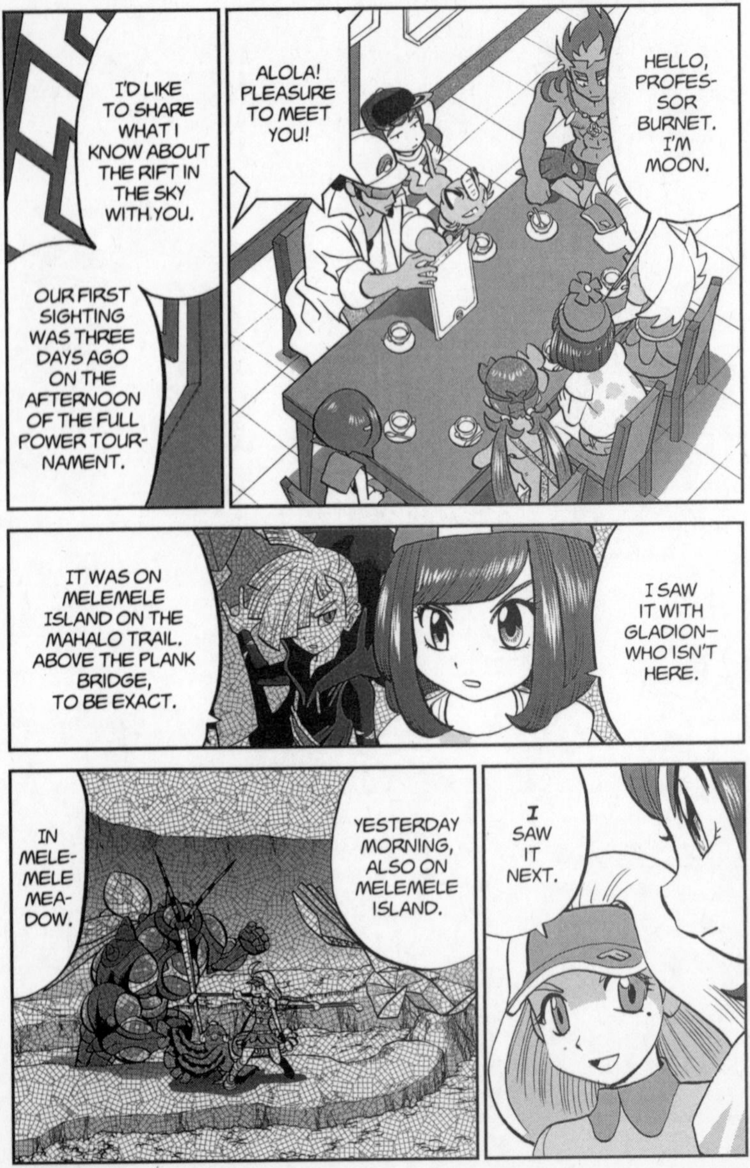
HELLO, PROFES-SOR BURNET. I'M MOON.
ALOLA! PLEASURE TO MEET YOU!
I'D LIKE TO SHARE WHAT I KNOW ABOUT THE RIFT IN THE SKY WITH YOU.
OUR FIRST SIGHTING WAS THREE DAYS AGO ON THE AFTERNOON OF THE FULL POWER TOUR-NAMENT.
I SAW IT WITH GLADION— WHO ISN'T HERE.
IT WAS ON MELEMELE ISLAND ON THE MAHALO TRAIL. ABOVE THE PLANK BRIDGE, TO BE EXACT.
I SAW IT NEXT.
YESTERDAY MORNING, ALSO ON MELEMELE ISLAND.
IN MELE-MELE MEA-DOW.

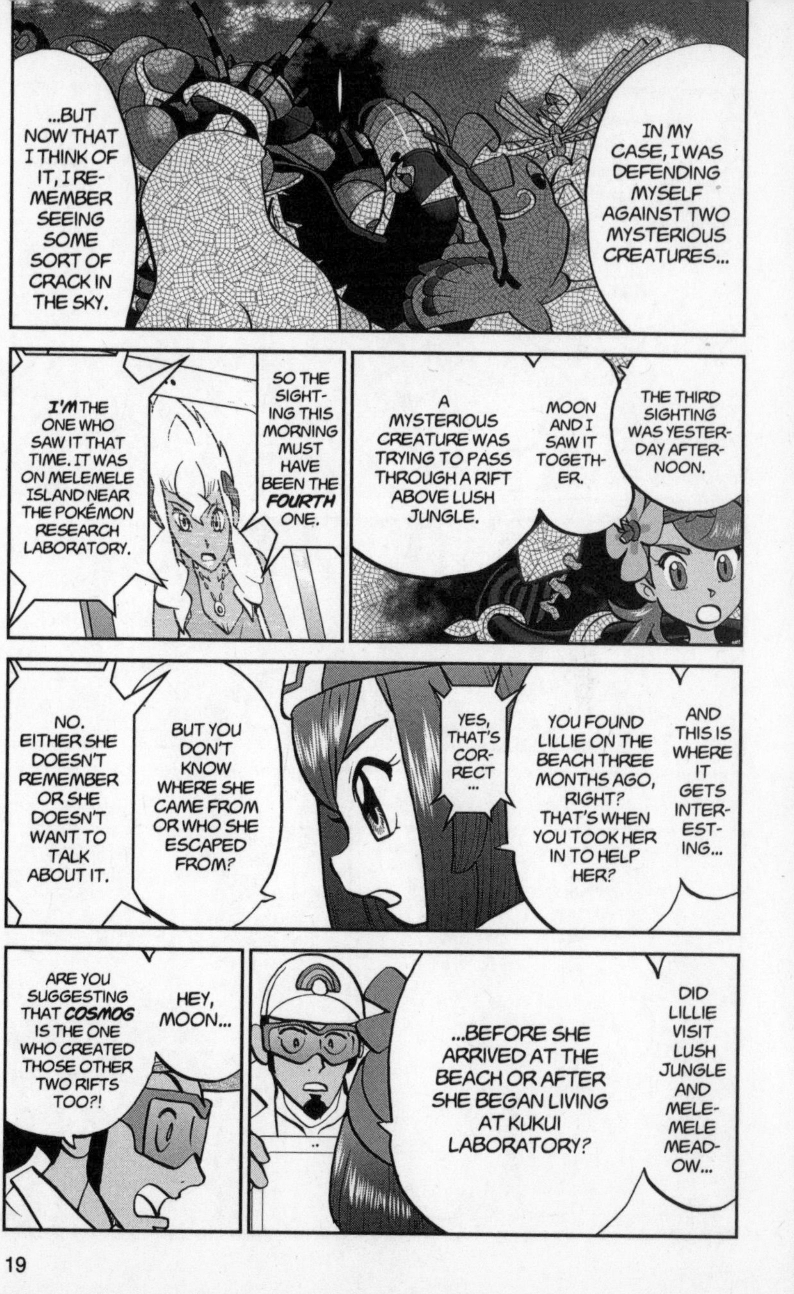
IN MY CASE, I WAS DEFENDING MYSELF AGAINST TWO MYSTERIOUS CREATURES...
...BUT NOW THAT I THINK OF IT, I REMEMBER SEEING SOME SORT OF CRACK IN THE SKY.
THE THIRD SIGHTING WAS YESTERDAY AFTERNOON.
MOON AND I SAW IT TOGETHER.
A MYSTERIOUS CREATURE WAS TRYING TO PASS THROUGH A RIFT ABOVE LUSH JUNGLE.
SO THE SIGHTING THIS MORNING MUST HAVE BEEN THE ***FOURTH*** ONE.
I'M THE ONE WHO SAW IT THAT TIME. IT WAS ON MELEMELE ISLAND NEAR THE POKÉMON RESEARCH LABORATORY.
AND THIS IS WHERE IT GETS INTERESTING...
YOU FOUND LILLIE ON THE BEACH THREE MONTHS AGO, RIGHT? THAT'S WHEN YOU TOOK HER IN TO HELP HER?
YES, THAT'S CORRECT...
BUT YOU DON'T KNOW WHERE SHE CAME FROM OR WHO SHE ESCAPED FROM?
NO. EITHER SHE DOESN'T REMEMBER OR SHE DOESN'T WANT TO TALK ABOUT IT.
DID LILLIE VISIT LUSH JUNGLE AND MELEMELE MEADOW...
...BEFORE SHE ARRIVED AT THE BEACH OR AFTER SHE BEGAN LIVING AT KUKUI LABORATORY?
HEY, MOON...
ARE YOU SUGGESTING THAT ***COSMOG*** IS THE ONE WHO CREATED THOSE OTHER TWO RIFTS TOO?!

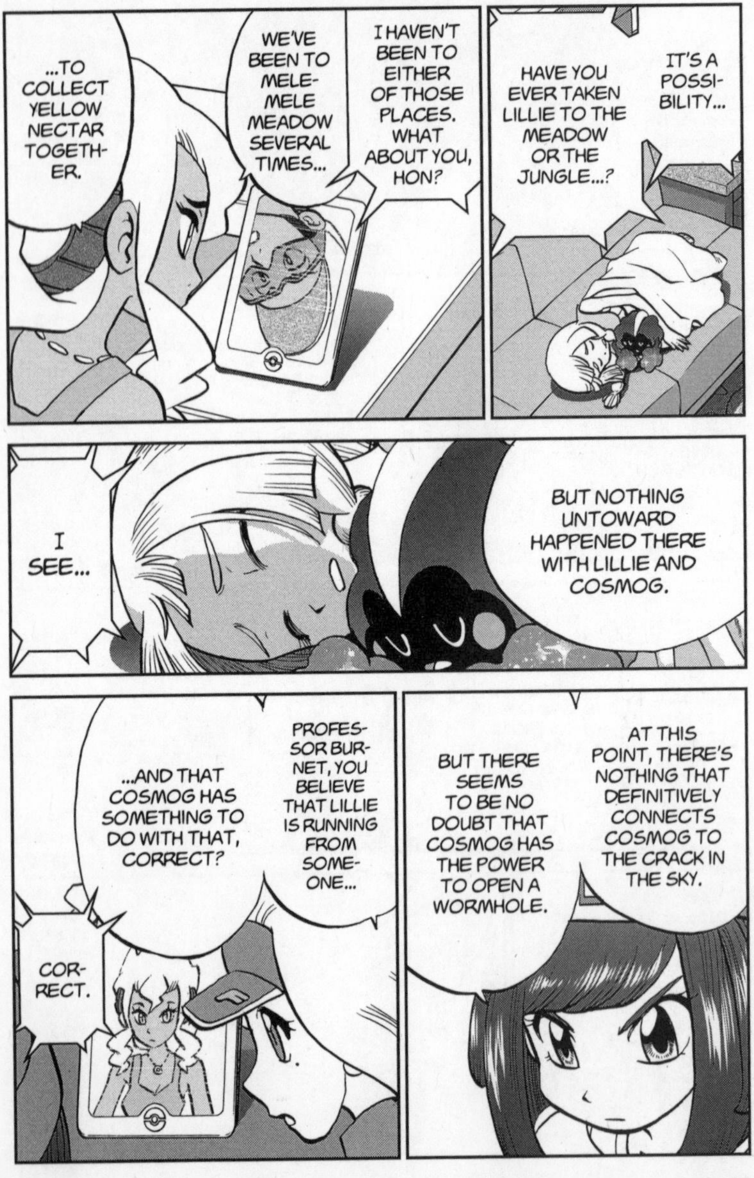
IT'S A POSSI-BILITY...
HAVE YOU EVER TAKEN LILLIE TO THE MEADOW OR THE JUNGLE...?
I HAVEN'T BEEN TO EITHER OF THOSE PLACES. WHAT ABOUT YOU, HON?
WE'VE BEEN TO MELE-MELE MEADOW SEVERAL TIMES...
...TO COLLECT YELLOW NECTAR TOGETH-ER.
BUT NOTHING UNTOWARD HAPPENED THERE WITH LILLIE AND COSMOG.
I SEE...
AT THIS POINT, THERE'S NOTHING THAT DEFINITIVELY CONNECTS COSMOG TO THE CRACK IN THE SKY.
BUT THERE SEEMS TO BE NO DOUBT THAT COSMOG HAS THE POWER TO OPEN A WORMHOLE.
PROFES-SOR BUR-NET, YOU BELIEVE THAT LILLIE IS RUNNING FROM SOME-ONE...
...AND THAT COSMOG HAS SOMETHING TO DO WITH THAT, CORRECT?
COR-RECT.

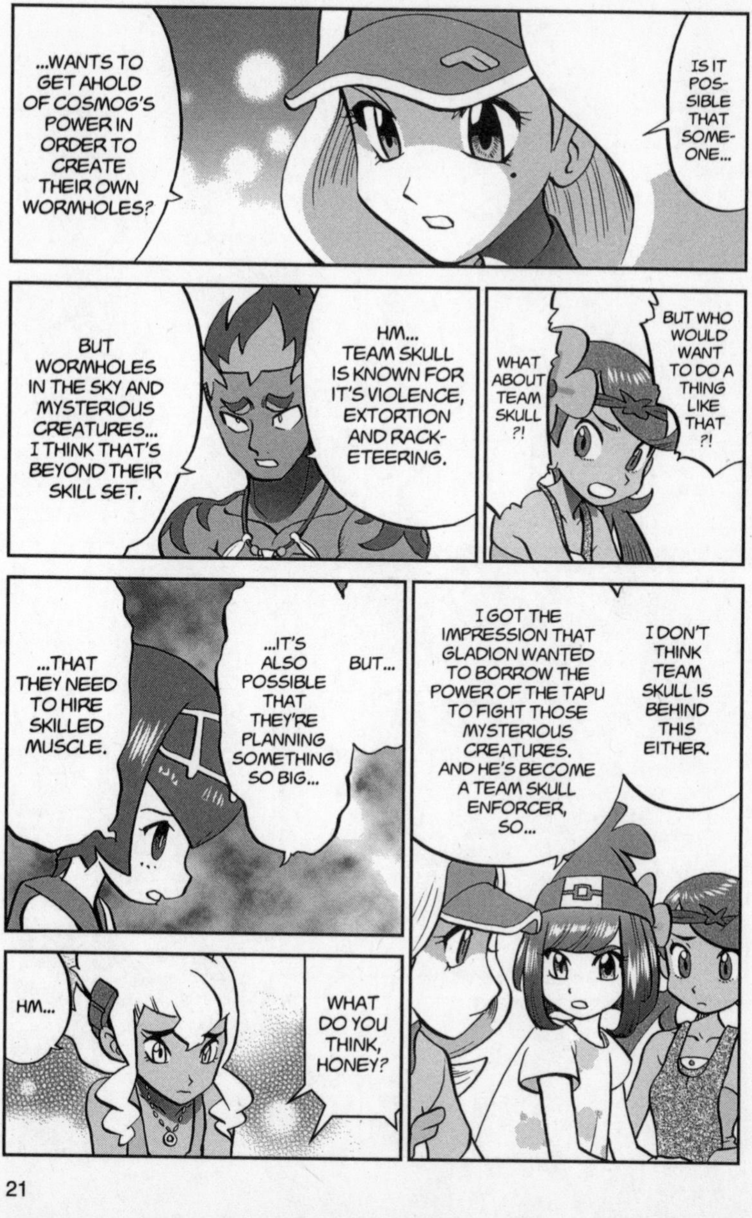
IS IT POS-SIBLE THAT SOME-ONE...
...WANTS TO GET AHOLD OF COSMOG'S POWER IN ORDER TO CREATE THEIR OWN WORMHOLES?
BUT WHO WOULD WANT TO DO A THING LIKE THAT?!
WHAT ABOUT TEAM SKULL?!
HM... TEAM SKULL IS KNOWN FOR IT'S VIOLENCE, EXTORTION AND RACK-ETEERING.
BUT WORMHOLES IN THE SKY AND MYSTERIOUS CREATURES... I THINK THAT'S BEYOND THEIR SKILL SET.
I DON'T THINK TEAM SKULL IS BEHIND THIS EITHER.
I GOT THE IMPRESSION THAT GLADION WANTED TO BORROW THE POWER OF THE TAPU TO FIGHT THOSE MYSTERIOUS CREATURES. AND HE'S BECOME A TEAM SKULL ENFORCER, SO...
BUT...
...IT'S ALSO POSSIBLE THAT THEY'RE PLANNING SOMETHING SO BIG...
...THAT THEY NEED TO HIRE SKILLED MUSCLE.
WHAT DO YOU THINK, HONEY?
HM...

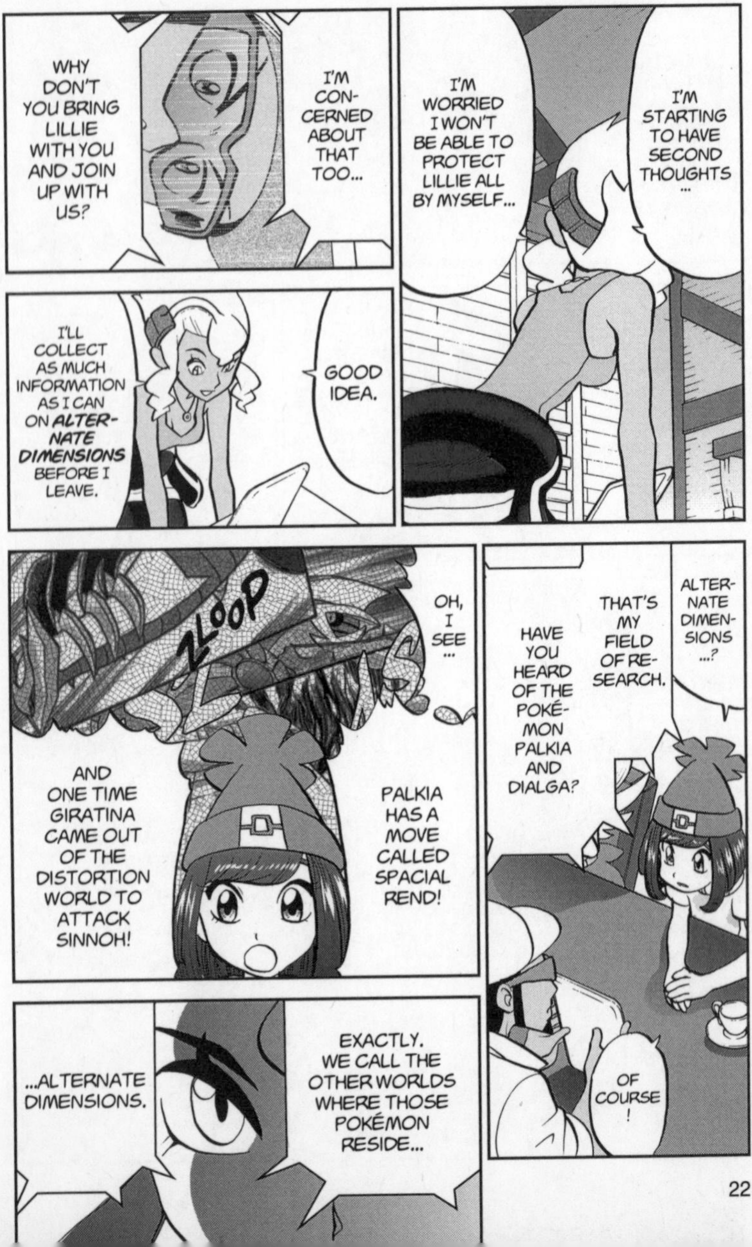
I'M STARTING TO HAVE SECOND THOUGHTS ...
I'M WORRIED I WON'T BE ABLE TO PROTECT LILLIE ALL BY MYSELF...
I'M CON-CERNED ABOUT THAT TOO...
WHY DON'T YOU BRING LILLIE WITH YOU AND JOIN UP WITH US?
GOOD IDEA.
I'LL COLLECT AS MUCH INFORMATION AS I CAN ON **ALTER-NATE DIMENSIONS** BEFORE I LEAVE.
ALTER-NATE DIMEN-SIONS ...?
THAT'S MY FIELD OF RE-SEARCH.
HAVE YOU HEARD OF THE POKÉ-MON PALKIA AND DIALGA?
OF COURSE !
OH, I SEE ...
ZLOOP
PALKIA HAS A MOVE CALLED SPACIAL REND!
AND ONE TIME GIRATINA CAME OUT OF THE DISTORTION WORLD TO ATTACK SINNOH!
EXACTLY. WE CALL THE OTHER WORLDS WHERE THOSE POKÉMON RESIDE...
...ALTERNATE DIMENSIONS.

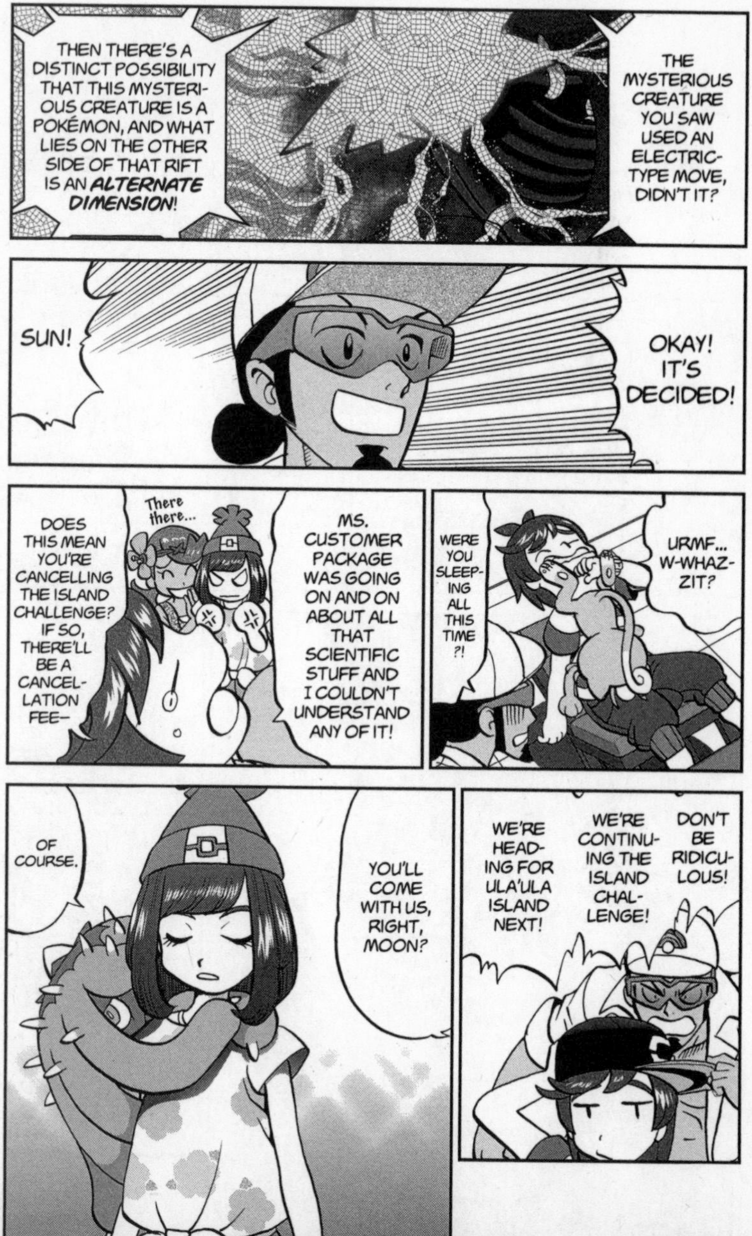
THE MYSTERIOUS CREATURE YOU SAW USED AN ELECTRIC-TYPE MOVE, DIDN'T IT?
THEN THERE'S A DISTINCT POSSIBILITY THAT THIS MYSTERIOUS CREATURE IS A POKÉMON, AND WHAT LIES ON THE OTHER SIDE OF THAT RIFT IS AN ***ALTERNATE DIMENSION***!
OKAY! IT'S DECIDED!
SUN!
URMF... W-WHAZZIT?
WERE YOU SLEEPING ALL THIS TIME?!
MS. CUSTOMER PACKAGE WAS GOING ON AND ON ABOUT ALL THAT SCIENTIFIC STUFF AND I COULDN'T UNDERSTAND ANY OF IT!
There there...
DOES THIS MEAN YOU'RE CANCELLING THE ISLAND CHALLENGE? IF SO, THERE'LL BE A CANCELLATION FEE–
DON'T BE RIDICULOUS!
WE'RE CONTINUING THE ISLAND CHALLENGE!
WE'RE HEADING FOR ULA'ULA ISLAND NEXT!
YOU'LL COME WITH US, RIGHT, MOON?
OF COURSE.

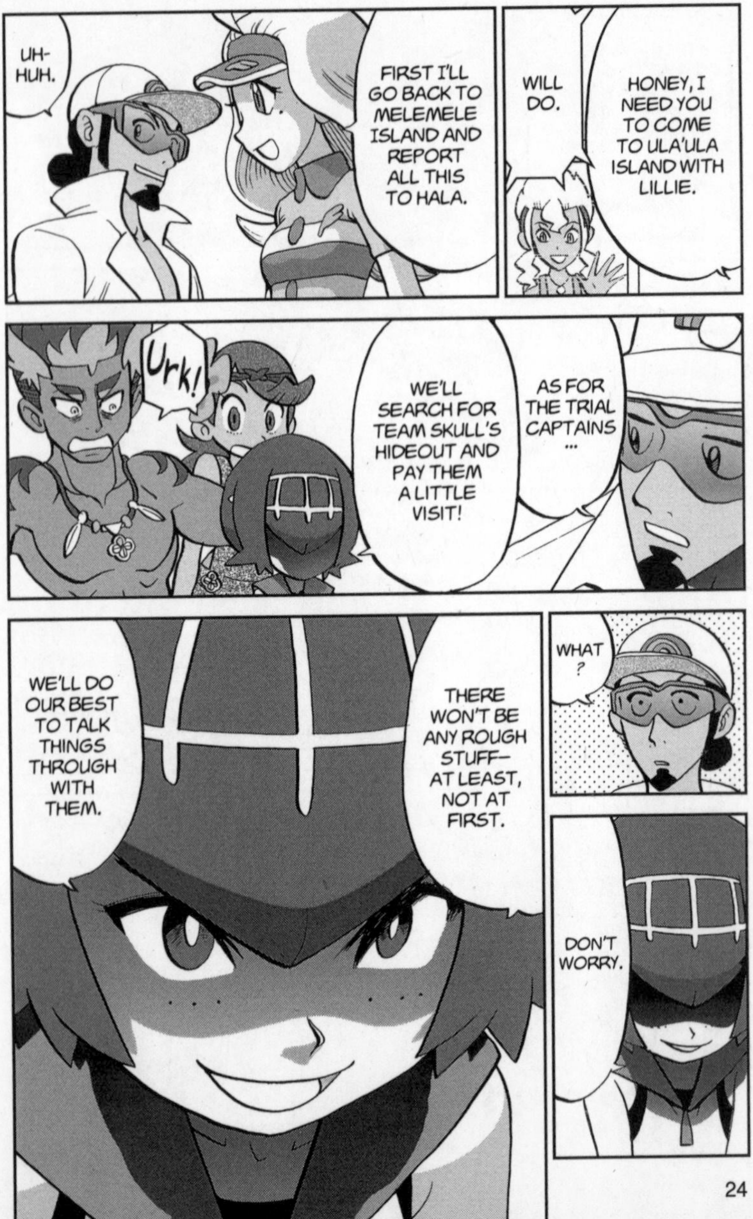

HONEY, I NEED YOU TO COME TO ULA'ULA ISLAND WITH LILLIE.
WILL DO.
FIRST I'LL GO BACK TO MELEMELE ISLAND AND REPORT ALL THIS TO HALA.
UH-HUH.
AS FOR THE TRIAL CAPTAINS ...
WE'LL SEARCH FOR TEAM SKULL'S HIDEOUT AND PAY THEM A LITTLE VISIT!
Urk!
WHAT?
DON'T WORRY.
THERE WON'T BE ANY ROUGH STUFF—AT LEAST, NOT AT FIRST.
WE'LL DO OUR BEST TO TALK THINGS THROUGH WITH THEM.

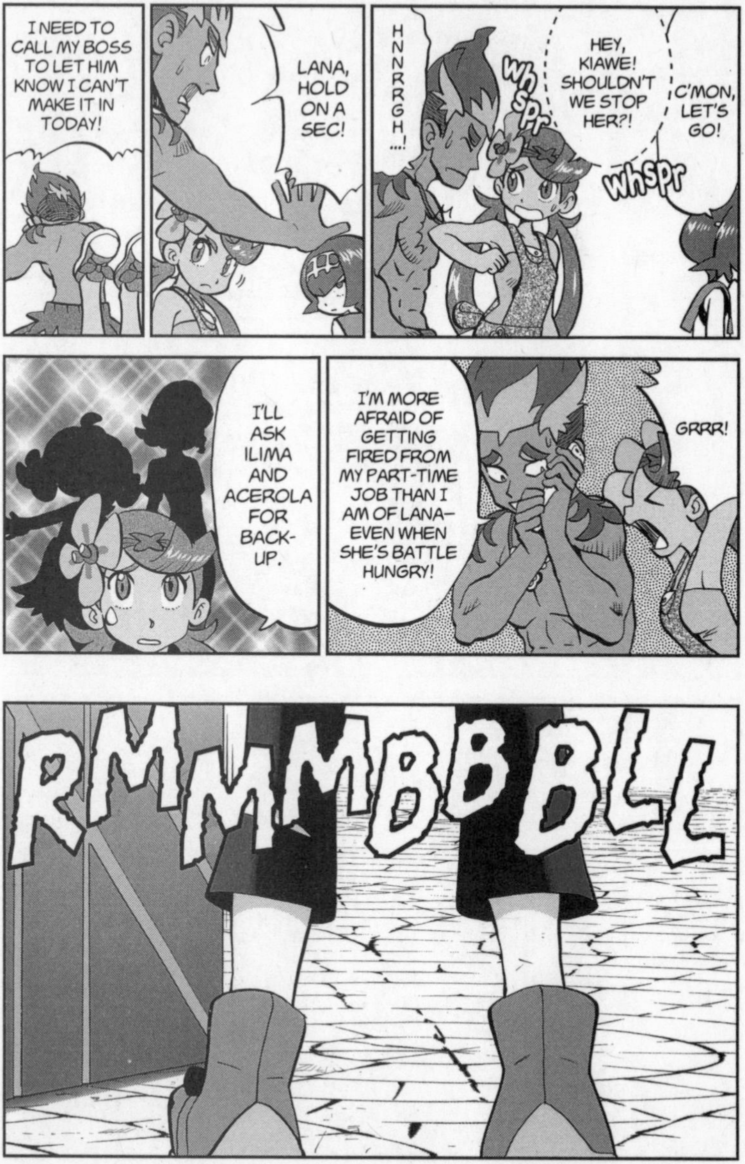
C'MON, LET'S GO!
HEY, KIAWE! SHOULDN'T WE STOP HER?!
whspr
whspr
HNNRRGH...!
LANA, HOLD ON A SEC!
I NEED TO CALL MY BOSS TO LET HIM KNOW I CAN'T MAKE IT IN TODAY!
GRRR!
I'M MORE AFRAID OF GETTING FIRED FROM MY PART-TIME JOB THAN I AM OF LANA—EVEN WHEN SHE'S BATTLE HUNGRY!
I'LL ASK ILIMA AND ACEROLA FOR BACK-UP.
RMMMBBBLL

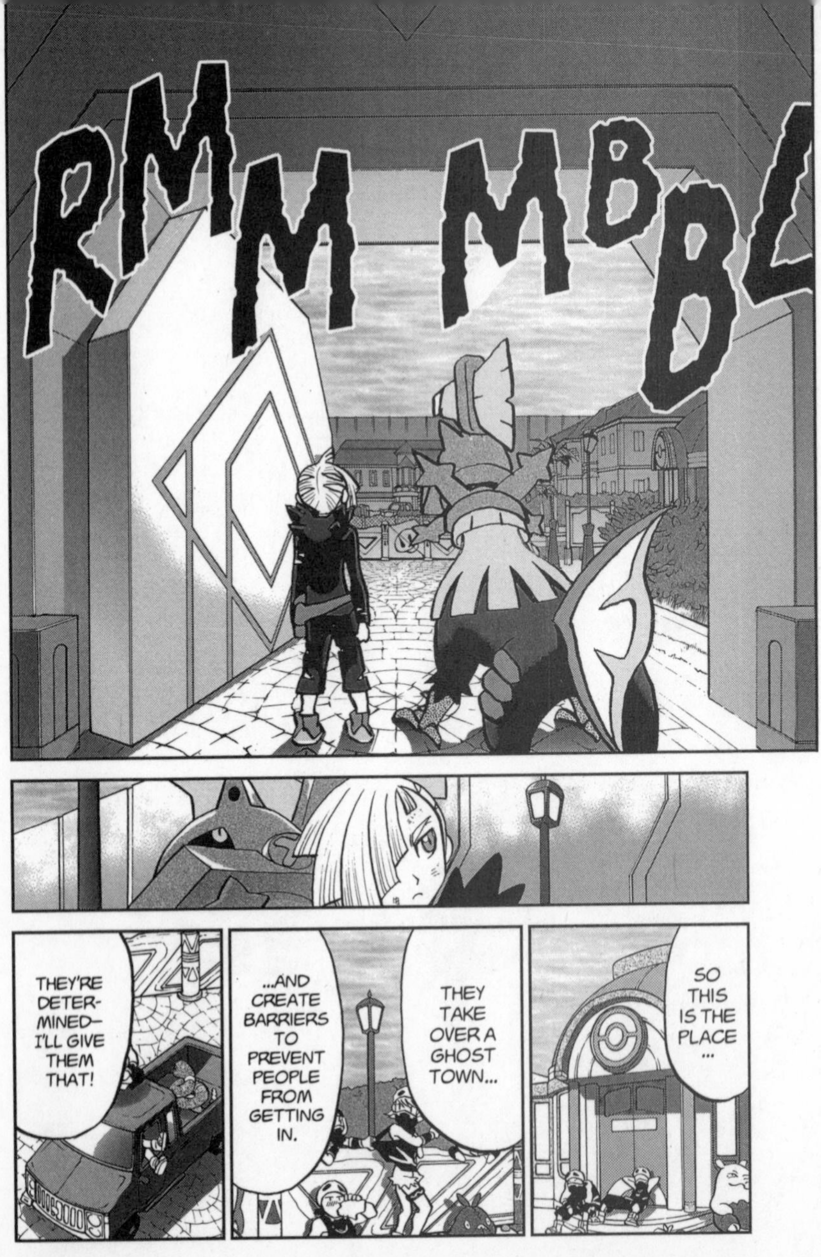
RMM MBB
SO THIS IS THE PLACE...
THEY TAKE OVER A GHOST TOWN...
...AND CREATE BARRIERS TO PREVENT PEOPLE FROM GETTING IN.
THEY'RE DETERMINED—I'LL GIVE THEM THAT!

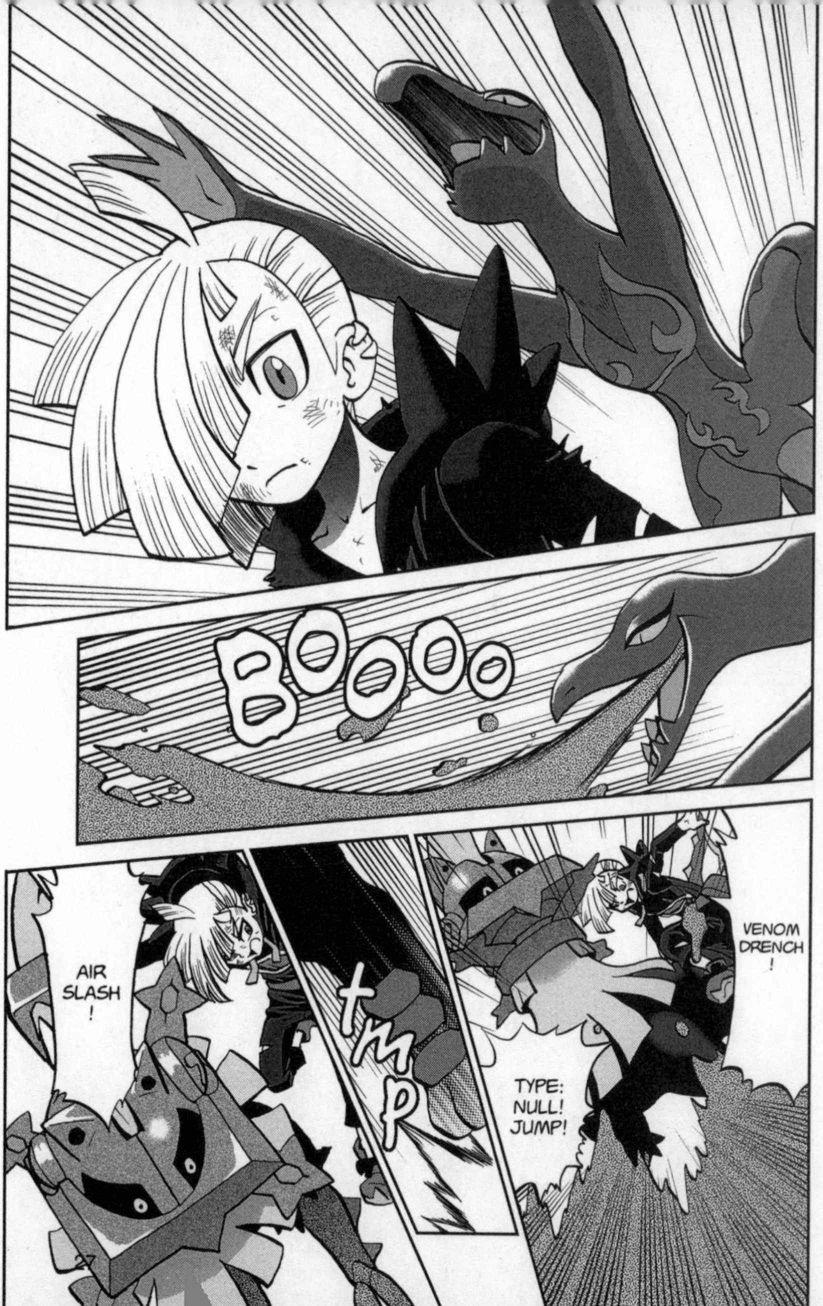
BOOOOO
VENOM DRENCH!
TYPE: NULL! JUMP!
tmp
AIR SLASH!

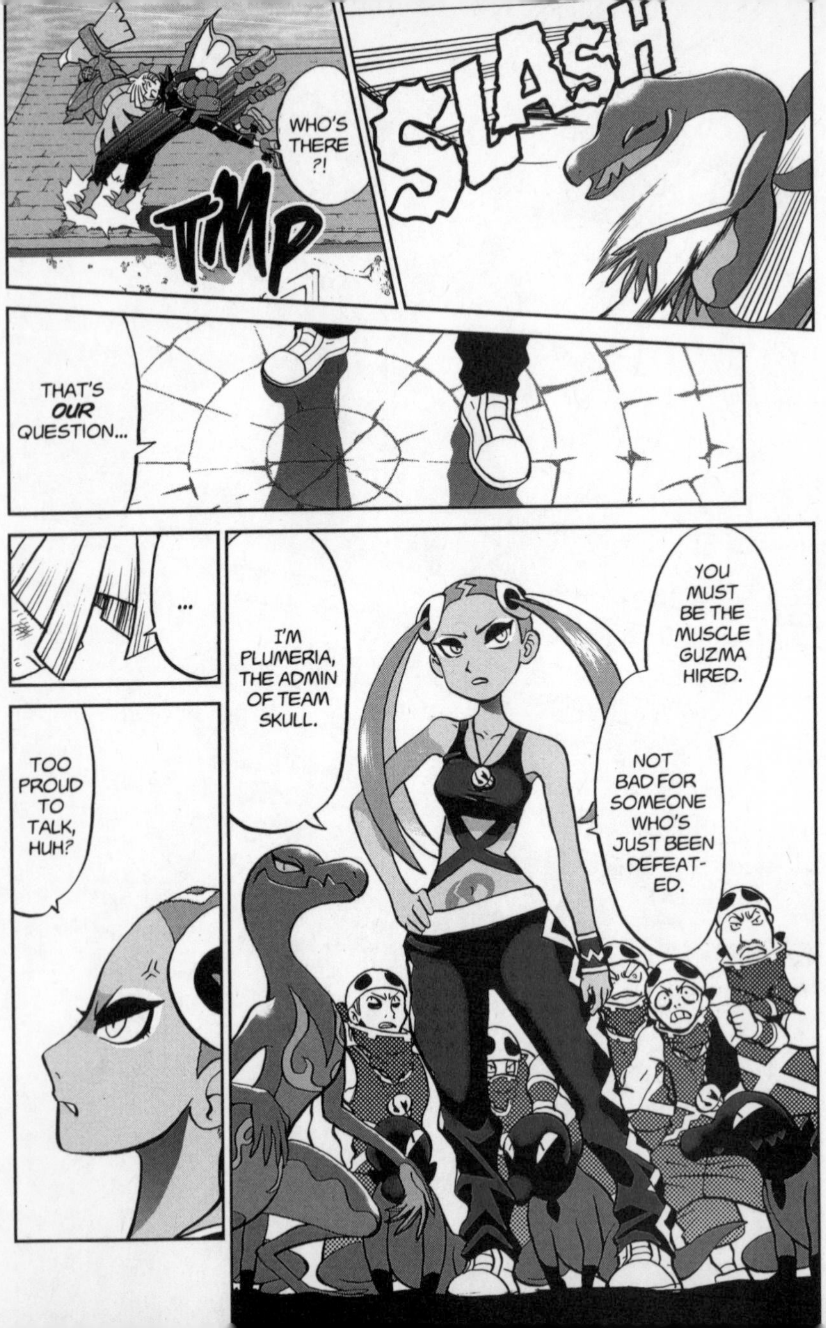
SLASH
WHO'S THERE ?!
TMP
THAT'S OUR QUESTION...
YOU MUST BE THE MUSCLE GUZMA HIRED.
I'M PLUMERIA, THE ADMIN OF TEAM SKULL.
NOT BAD FOR SOMEONE WHO'S JUST BEEN DEFEAT-ED.
...
TOO PROUD TO TALK, HUH?

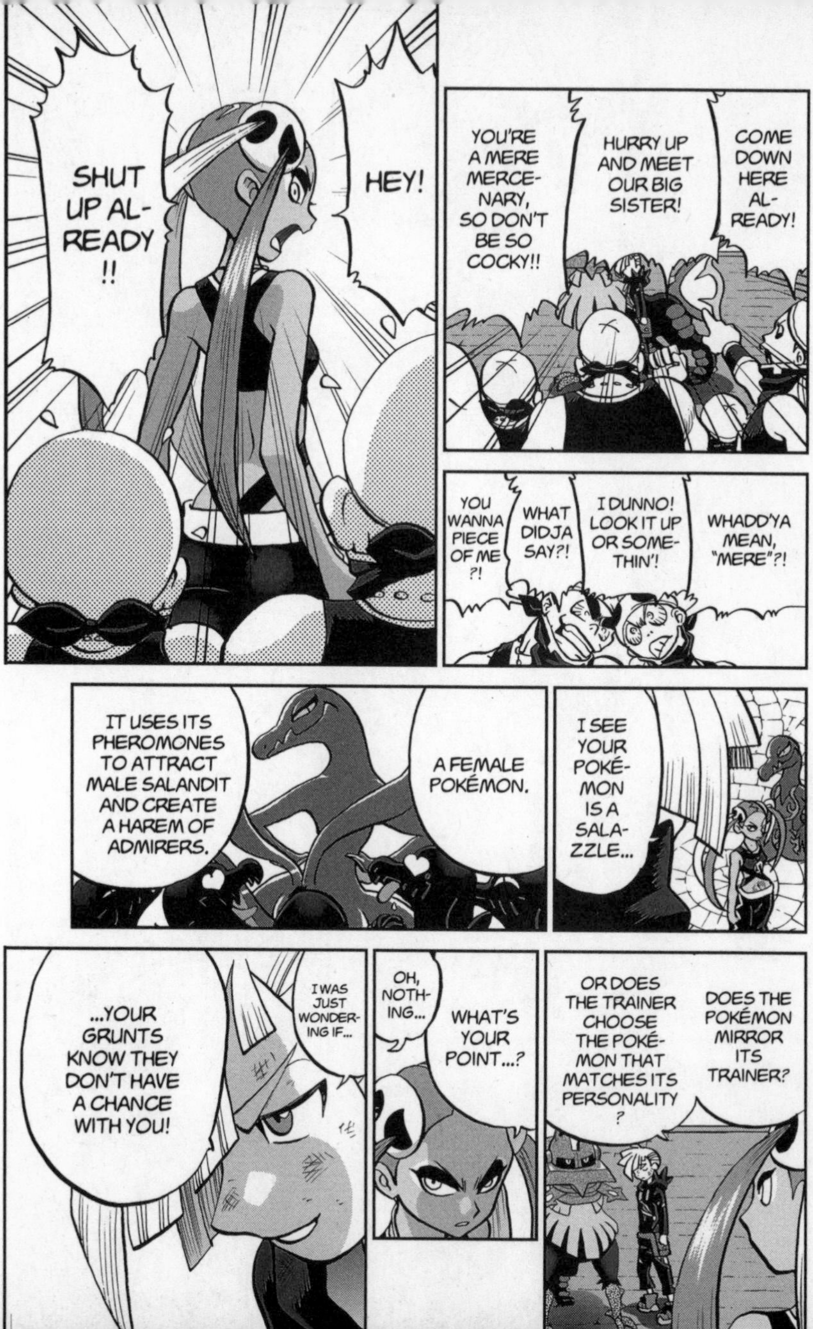
COME DOWN HERE ALREADY!
HURRY UP AND MEET OUR BIG SISTER!
YOU'RE A MERE MERCENARY, SO DON'T BE SO COCKY!!
WHADD'YA MEAN, "MERE"?!
I DUNNO! LOOK IT UP OR SOMETHIN'!
WHAT DIDJA SAY?!
YOU WANNA PIECE OF ME?!
HEY!
SHUT UP ALREADY!!
I SEE YOUR POKÉMON IS A SALAZZLE...
A FEMALE POKÉMON.
IT USES ITS PHEROMONES TO ATTRACT MALE SALANDIT AND CREATE A HAREM OF ADMIRERS.
DOES THE POKÉMON MIRROR ITS TRAINER?
OR DOES THE TRAINER CHOOSE THE POKÉMON THAT MATCHES ITS PERSONALITY?
WHAT'S YOUR POINT...?
OH, NOTHING...
I WAS JUST WONDERING IF...
...YOUR GRUNTS KNOW THEY DON'T HAVE A CHANCE WITH YOU!

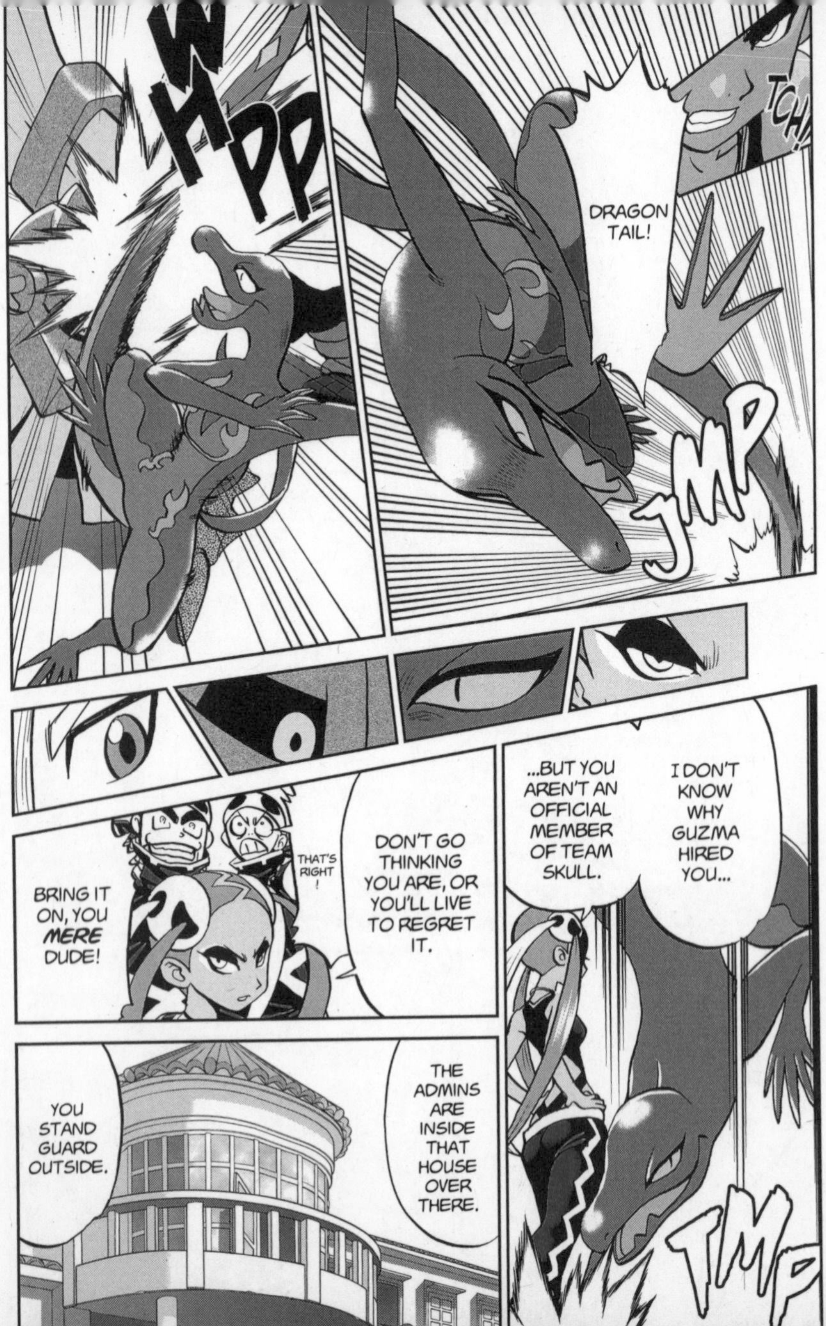
TCH!
DRAGON TAIL!
JMP
WHPP
I DON'T KNOW WHY GUZMA HIRED YOU...
...BUT YOU AREN'T AN OFFICIAL MEMBER OF TEAM SKULL.
TMP
DON'T GO THINKING YOU ARE, OR YOU'LL LIVE TO REGRET IT.
THAT'S RIGHT!
BRING IT ON, YOU *MERE* DUDE!
THE ADMINS ARE INSIDE THAT HOUSE OVER THERE.
YOU STAND GUARD OUTSIDE.

sh ff

FOLLOW ME.

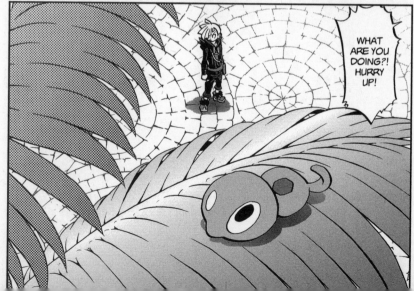

WHAT ARE YOU DOING?! HURRY UP!

Tapu

The Legendary Pokémon who protect the four islands of Alola. Ula'ula, Akala, Melemele and Poni each have one Tapu. Although they are Island Guardians, they can be whimsical and mischievous at times.

Guide to Alola 12

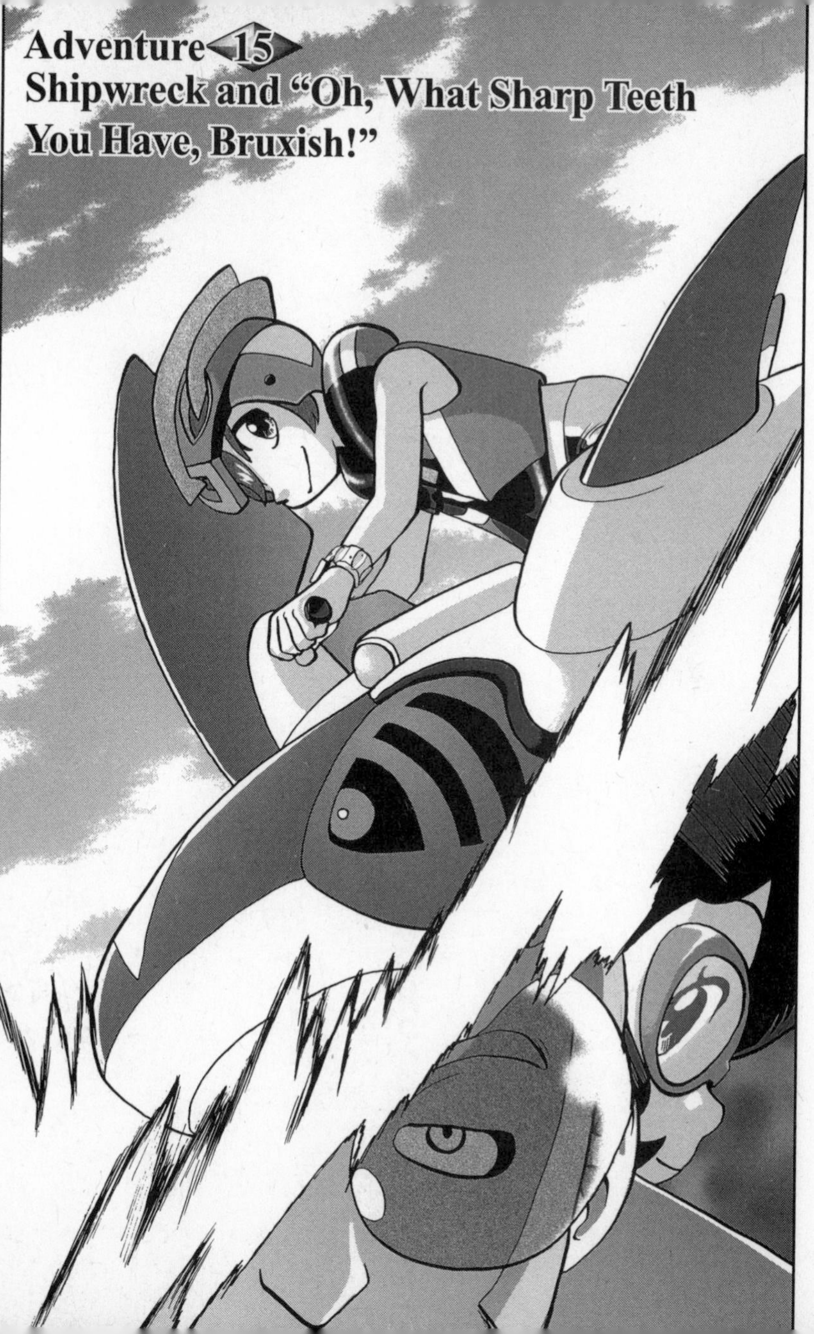
Adventure 15
Shipwreck and "Oh, What Sharp Teeth You Have, Bruxish!"

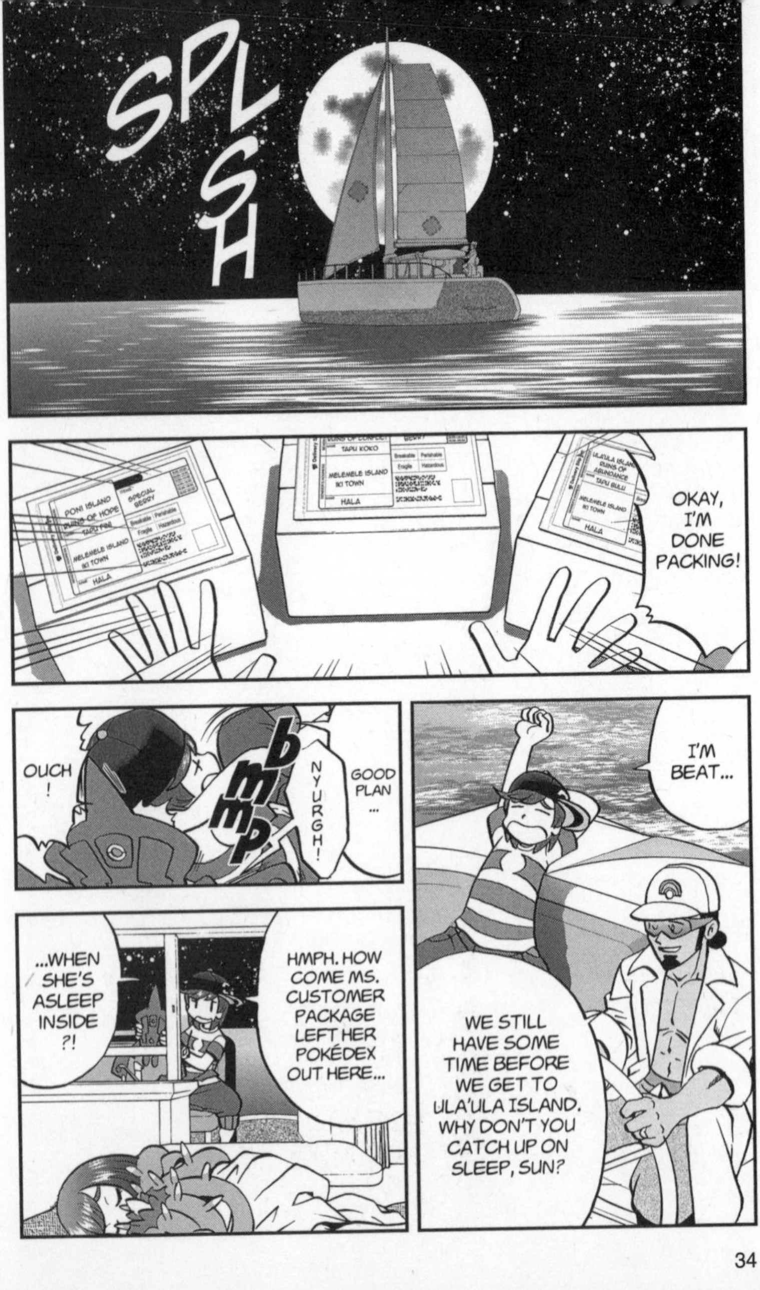
SPLSH
OKAY, I'M DONE PACKING!
I'M BEAT...
WE STILL HAVE SOME TIME BEFORE WE GET TO ULA'ULA ISLAND. WHY DON'T YOU CATCH UP ON SLEEP, SUN?
GOOD PLAN...
NYURGH!
bmmp
OUCH!
HMPH. HOW COME MS. CUSTOMER PACKAGE LEFT HER POKÉDEX OUT HERE...
...WHEN SHE'S ASLEEP INSIDE?!

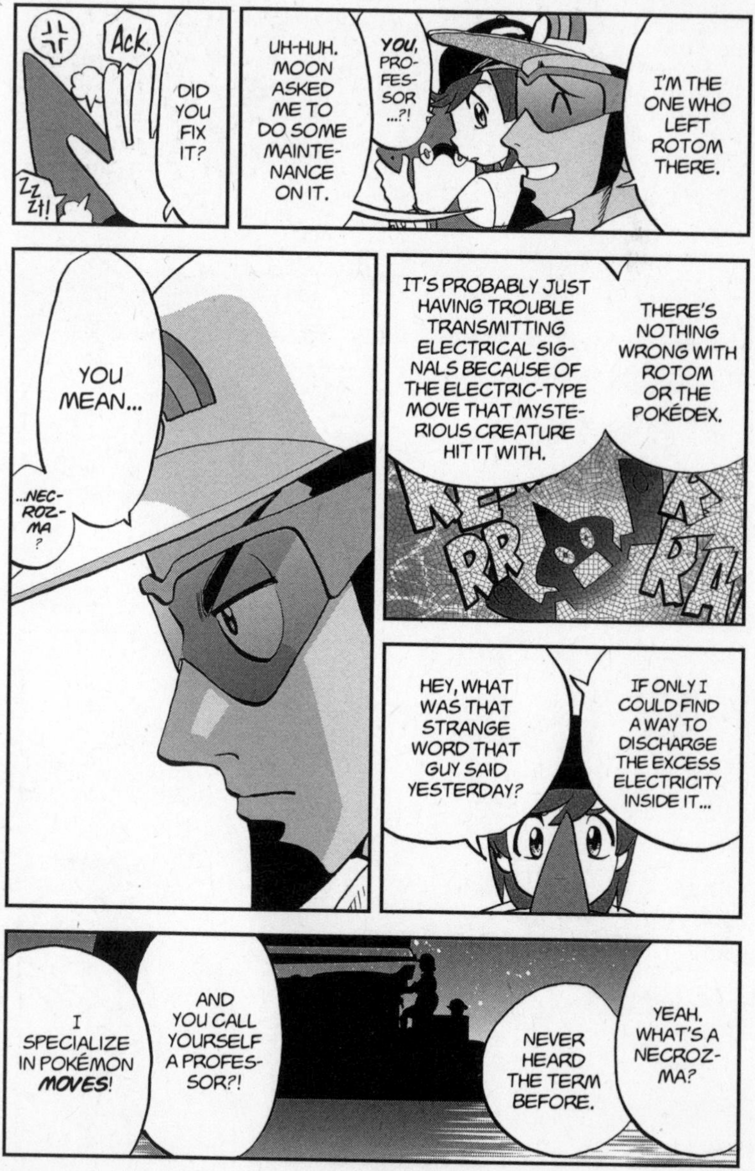
I'M THE ONE WHO LEFT ROTOM THERE.
YOU, PROFESSOR...?!
UH-HUH. MOON ASKED ME TO DO SOME MAINTENANCE ON IT.
DID YOU FIX IT?
Ack.
ZZ ZT!
THERE'S NOTHING WRONG WITH ROTOM OR THE POKÉDEX.
IT'S PROBABLY JUST HAVING TROUBLE TRANSMITTING ELECTRICAL SIGNALS BECAUSE OF THE ELECTRIC-TYPE MOVE THAT MYSTERIOUS CREATURE HIT IT WITH.
IF ONLY I COULD FIND A WAY TO DISCHARGE THE EXCESS ELECTRICITY INSIDE IT...
HEY, WHAT WAS THAT STRANGE WORD THAT GUY SAID YESTERDAY?
YOU MEAN...
...NECROZMA?
YEAH. WHAT'S A NECROZMA?
NEVER HEARD THE TERM BEFORE.
AND YOU CALL YOURSELF A PROFESSOR?!
I SPECIALIZE IN POKÉMON *MOVES*!

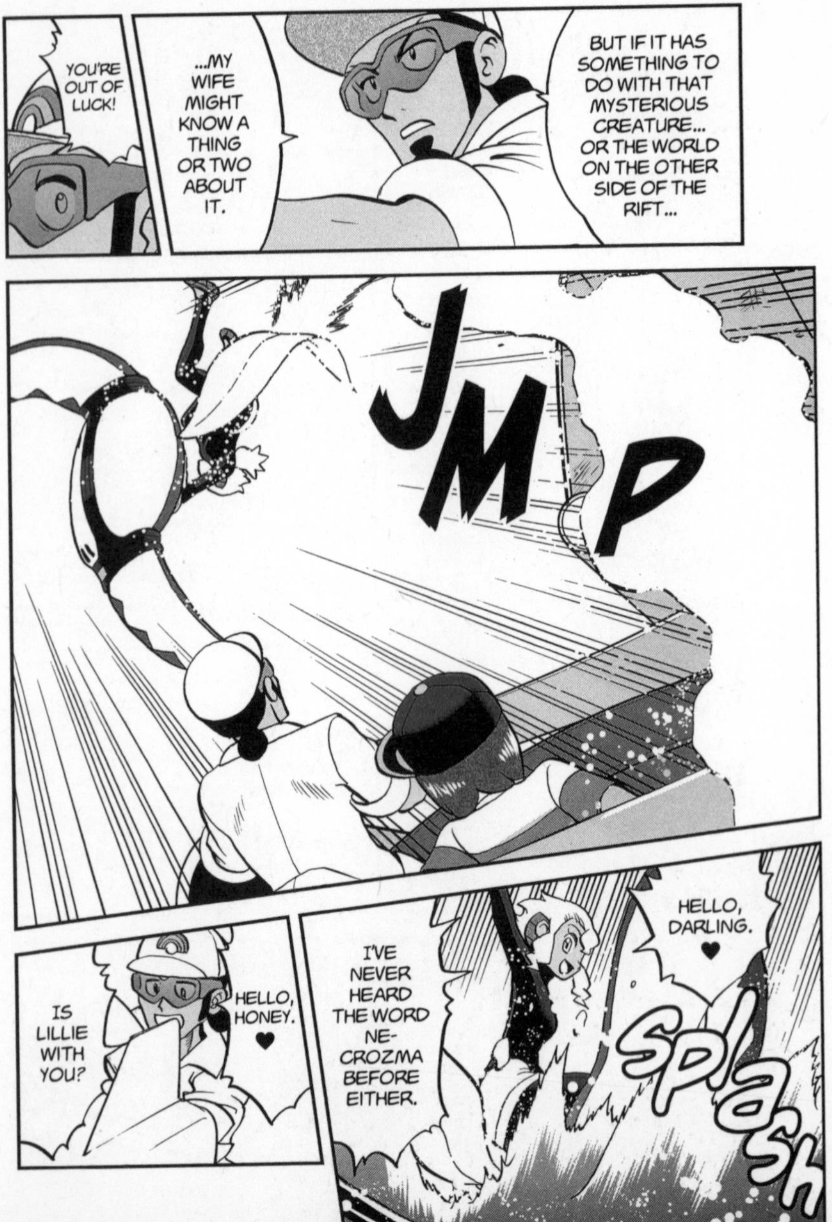
BUT IF IT HAS SOMETHING TO DO WITH THAT MYSTERIOUS CREATURE... OR THE WORLD ON THE OTHER SIDE OF THE RIFT...
...MY WIFE MIGHT KNOW A THING OR TWO ABOUT IT.
YOU'RE OUT OF LUCK!
JMP
HELLO, DARLING. ♥
I'VE NEVER HEARD THE WORD NE-CROZMA BEFORE EITHER.
Splash
HELLO, HONEY. ♥
IS LILLIE WITH YOU?

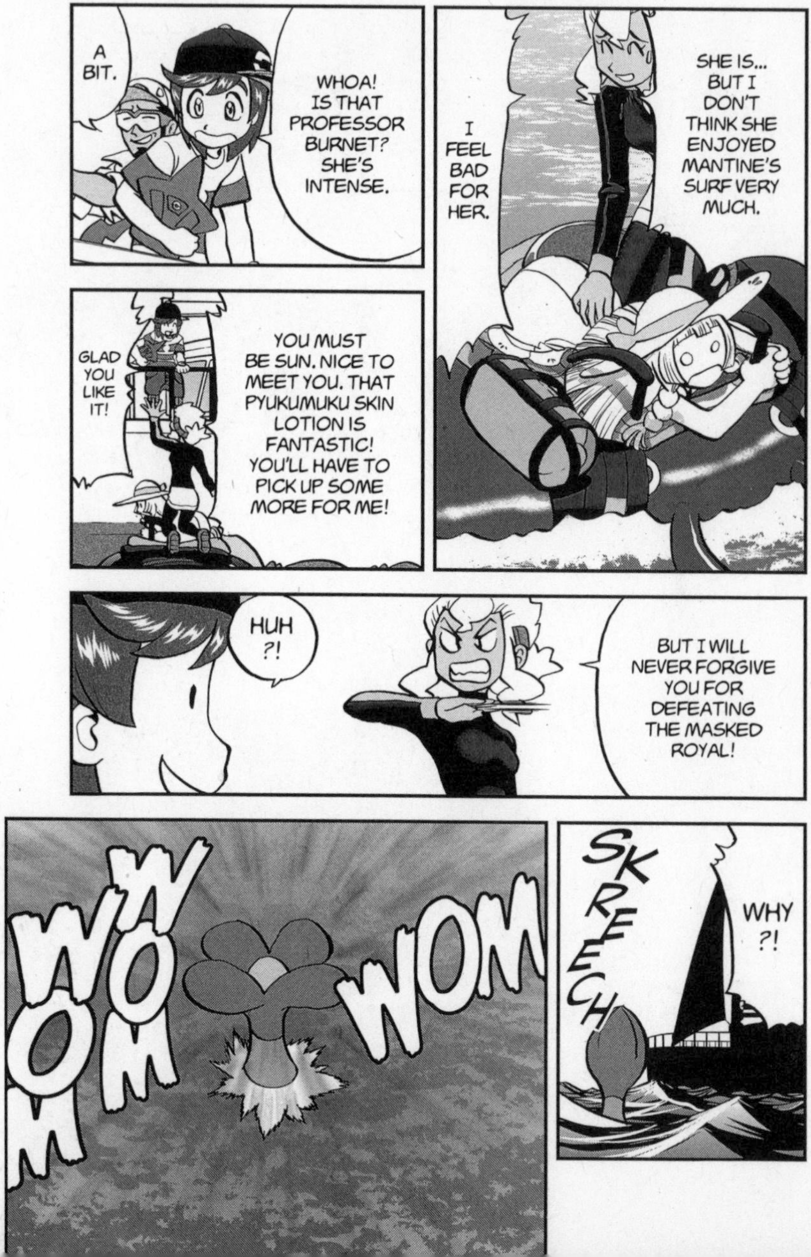
SHE IS... BUT I DON'T THINK SHE ENJOYED MANTINE'S SURF VERY MUCH.
I FEEL BAD FOR HER.
WHOA! IS THAT PROFESSOR BURNET? SHE'S INTENSE.
A BIT.
YOU MUST BE SUN. NICE TO MEET YOU. THAT PYUKUMUKU SKIN LOTION IS FANTASTIC! YOU'LL HAVE TO PICK UP SOME MORE FOR ME!
GLAD YOU LIKE IT!
BUT I WILL NEVER FORGIVE YOU FOR DEFEATING THE MASKED ROYAL!
HUH ?!
SKREECH
WHY ?!
WOM
WOM
WOM
WOM

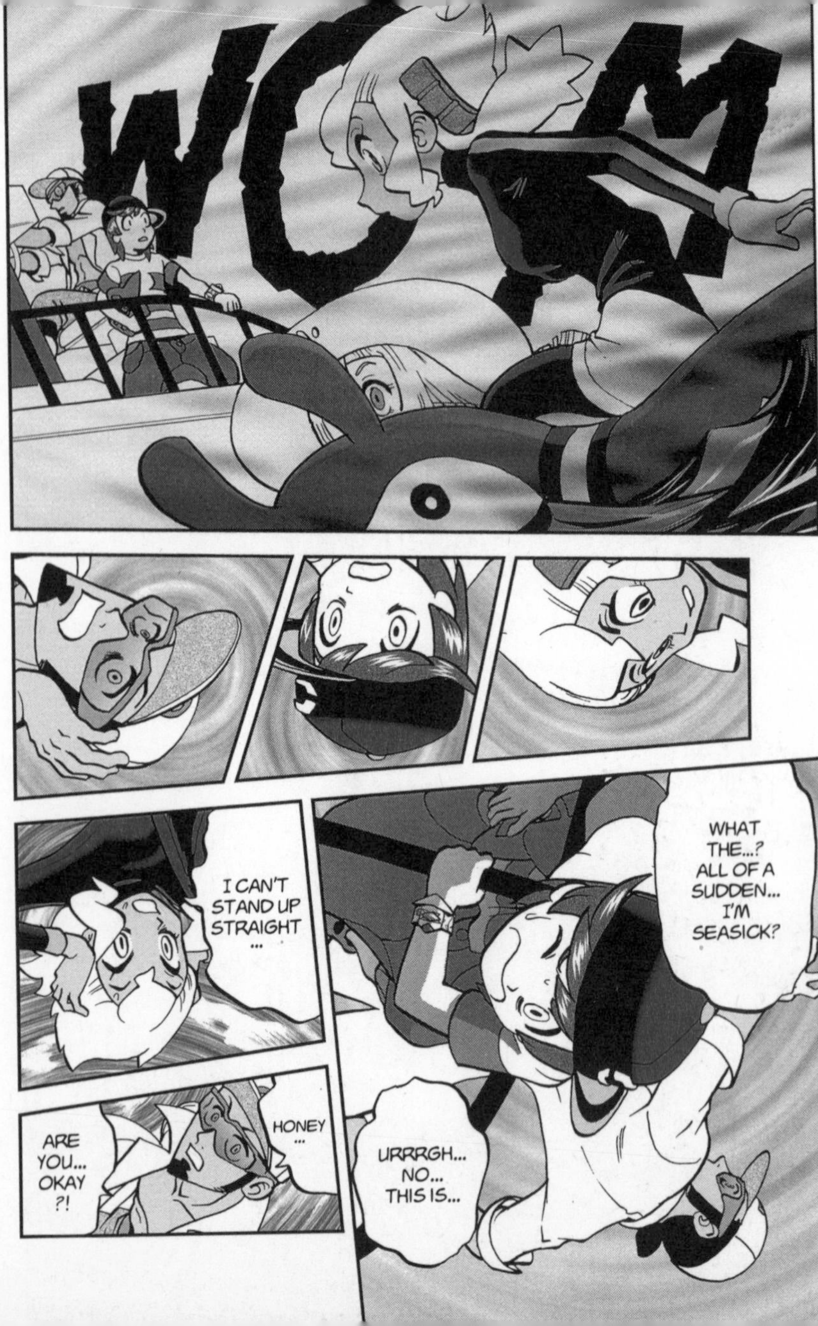
WOM
WHAT THE...? ALL OF A SUDDEN... I'M SEASICK?
URRRGH... NO... THIS IS...
I CAN'T STAND UP STRAIGHT ...
HONEY ...
ARE YOU... OKAY ?!

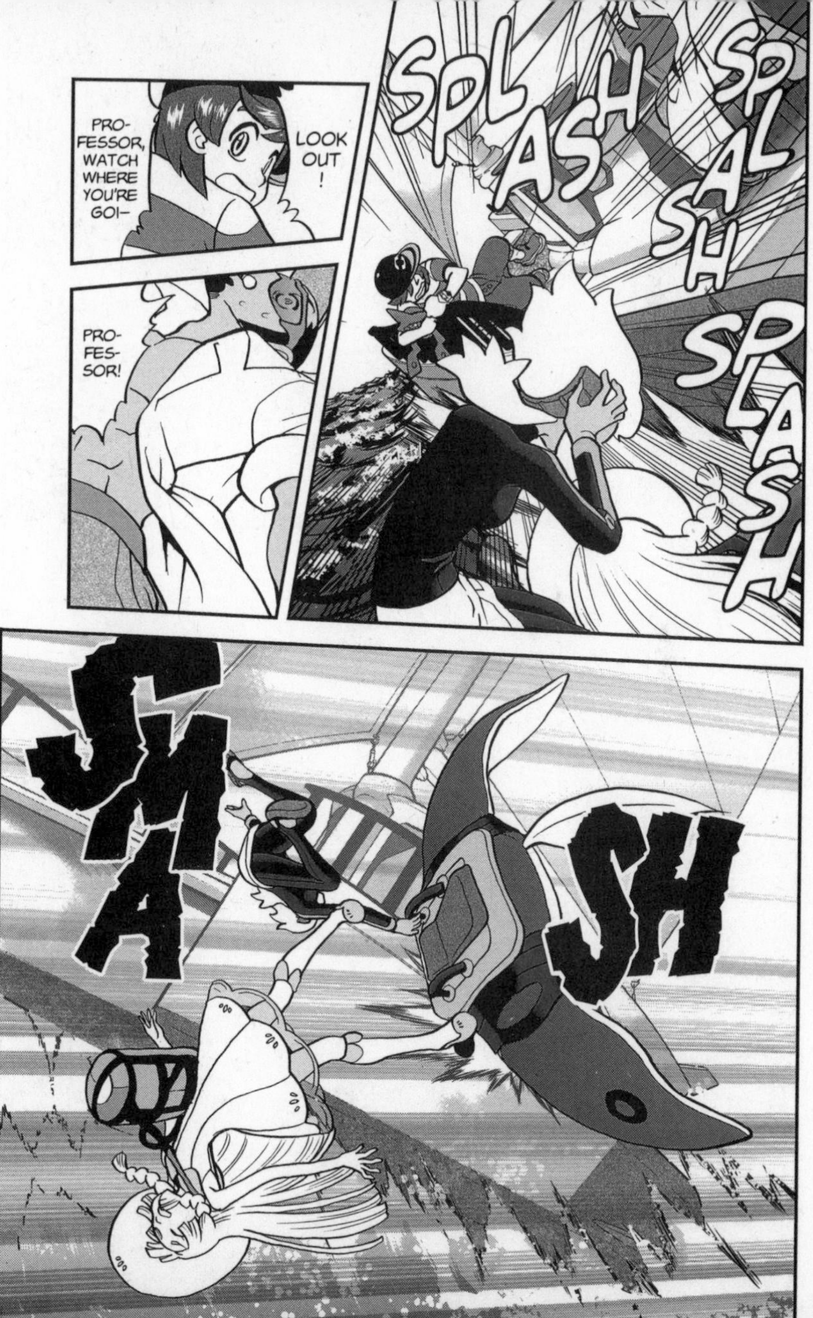
SPLASH
SPLASH
SPLASH
LOOK OUT!
PROFESSOR, WATCH WHERE YOU'RE GOI—
PROFESSOR!
SMASH

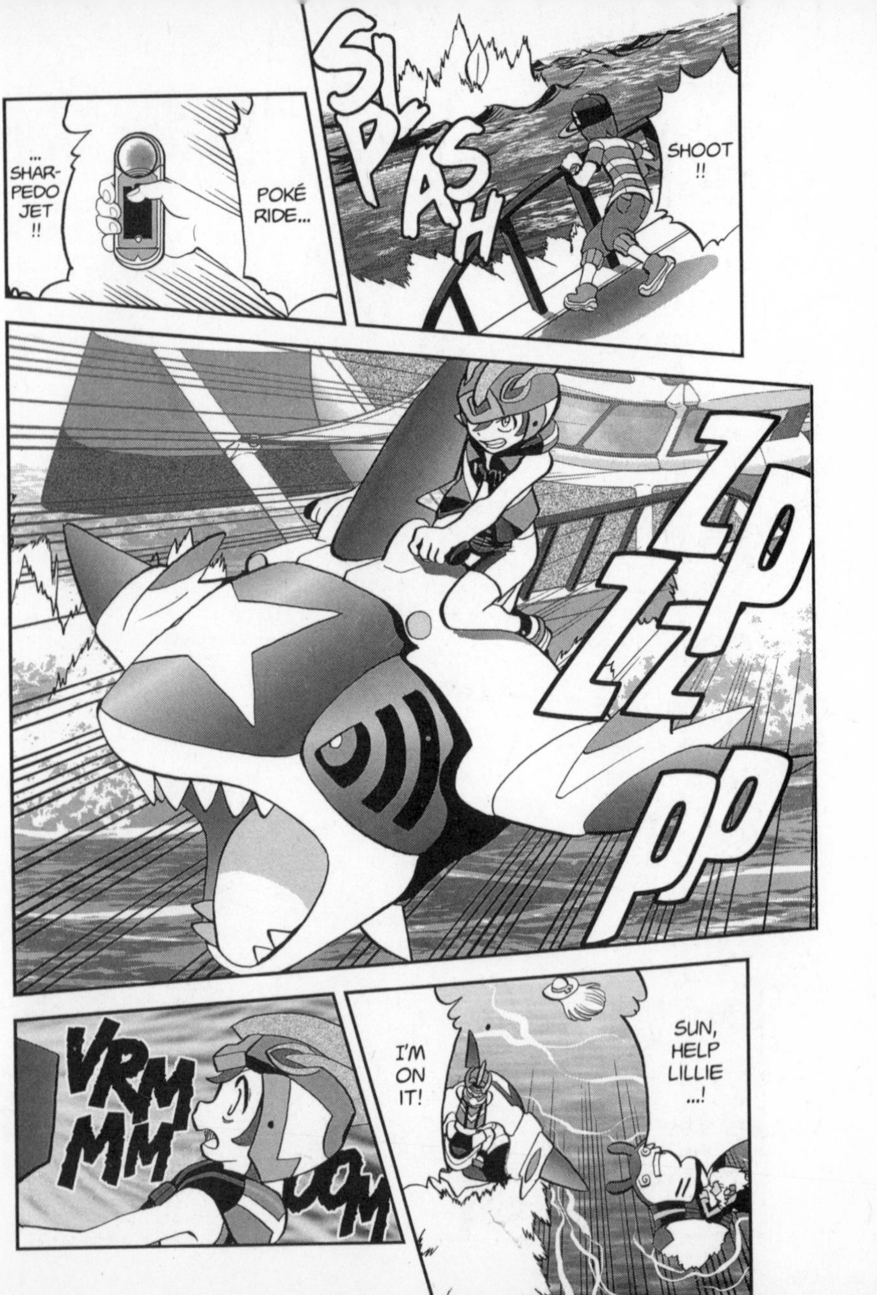
SPLASH
SHOOT!!
POKÉ RIDE...
...SHARPEDO JET!!
SUN, HELP LILLIE ...!
I'M ON IT!
VRMMM

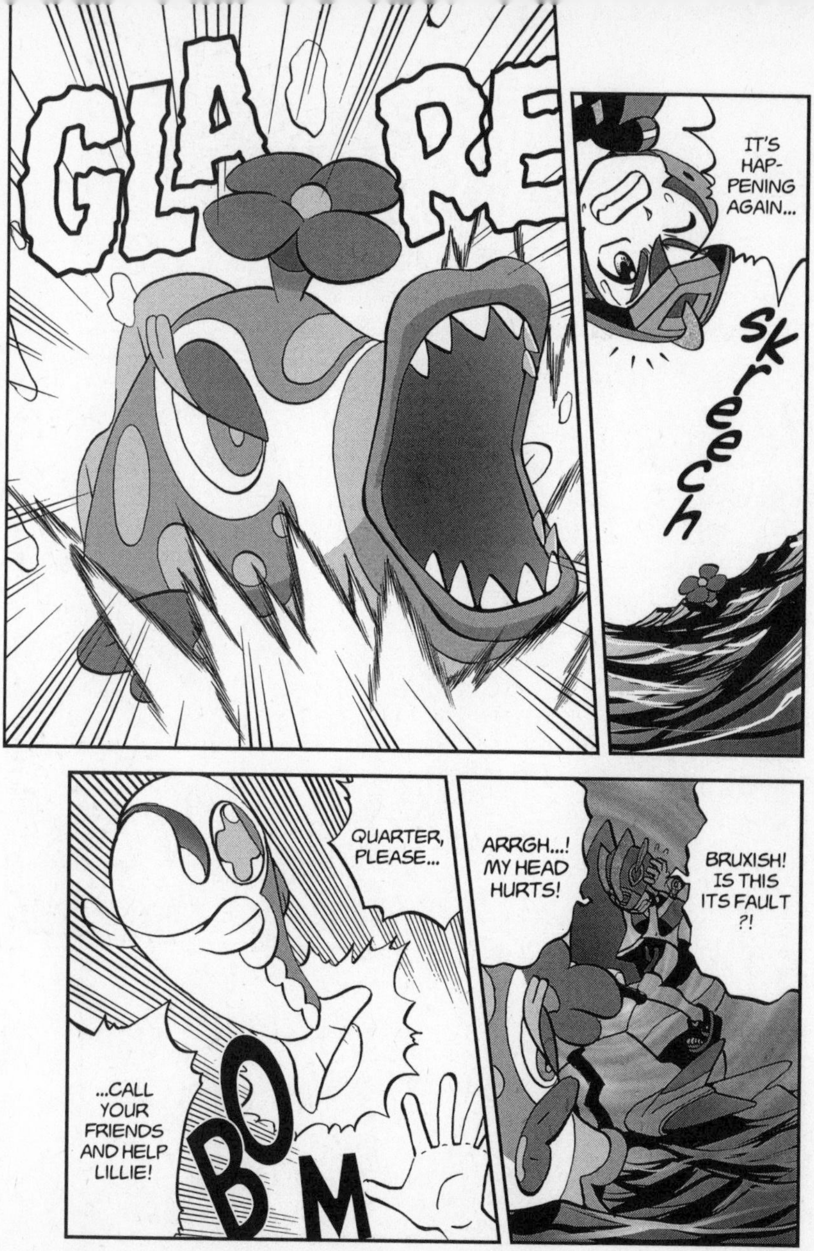
IT'S HAP-PENING AGAIN...
skreeech
GLARE
BRUXISH! IS THIS ITS FAULT ?!
ARRGH...! MY HEAD HURTS!
QUARTER, PLEASE...
...CALL YOUR FRIENDS AND HELP LILLIE!
BOOM

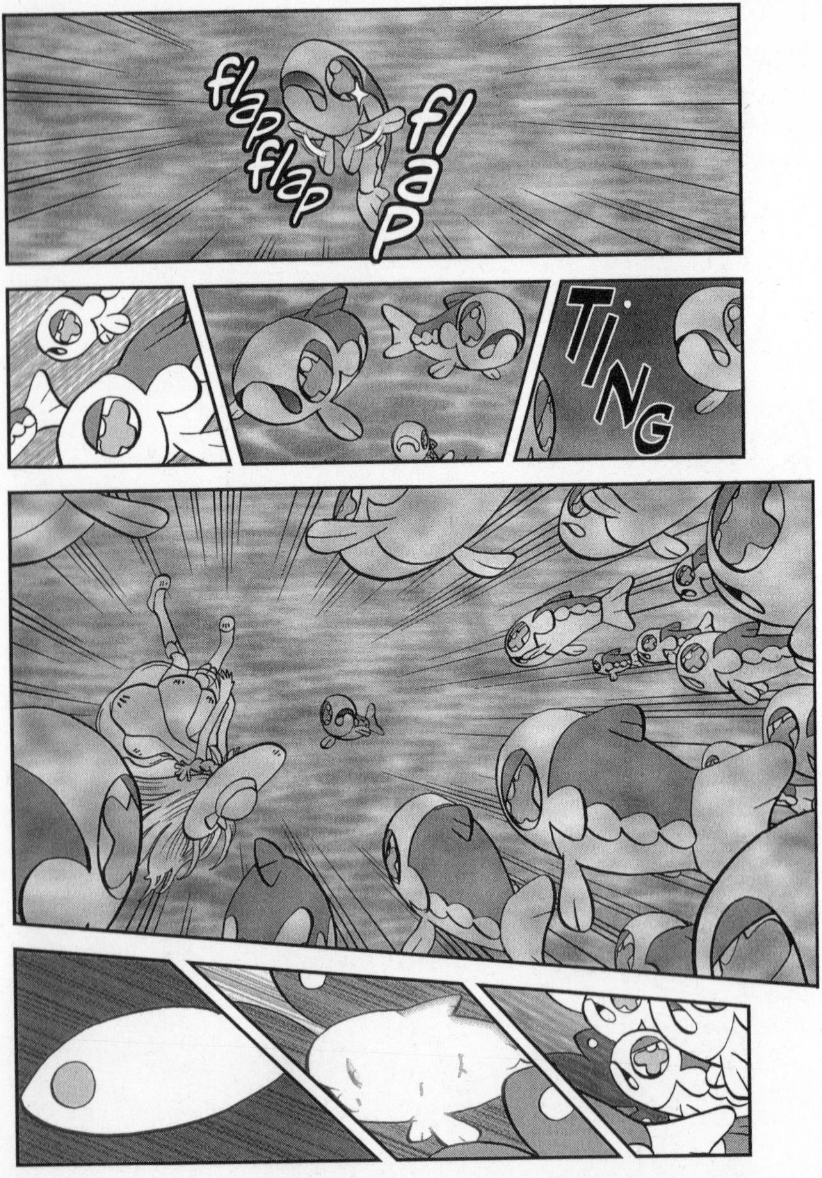
flap
flapflap
TING

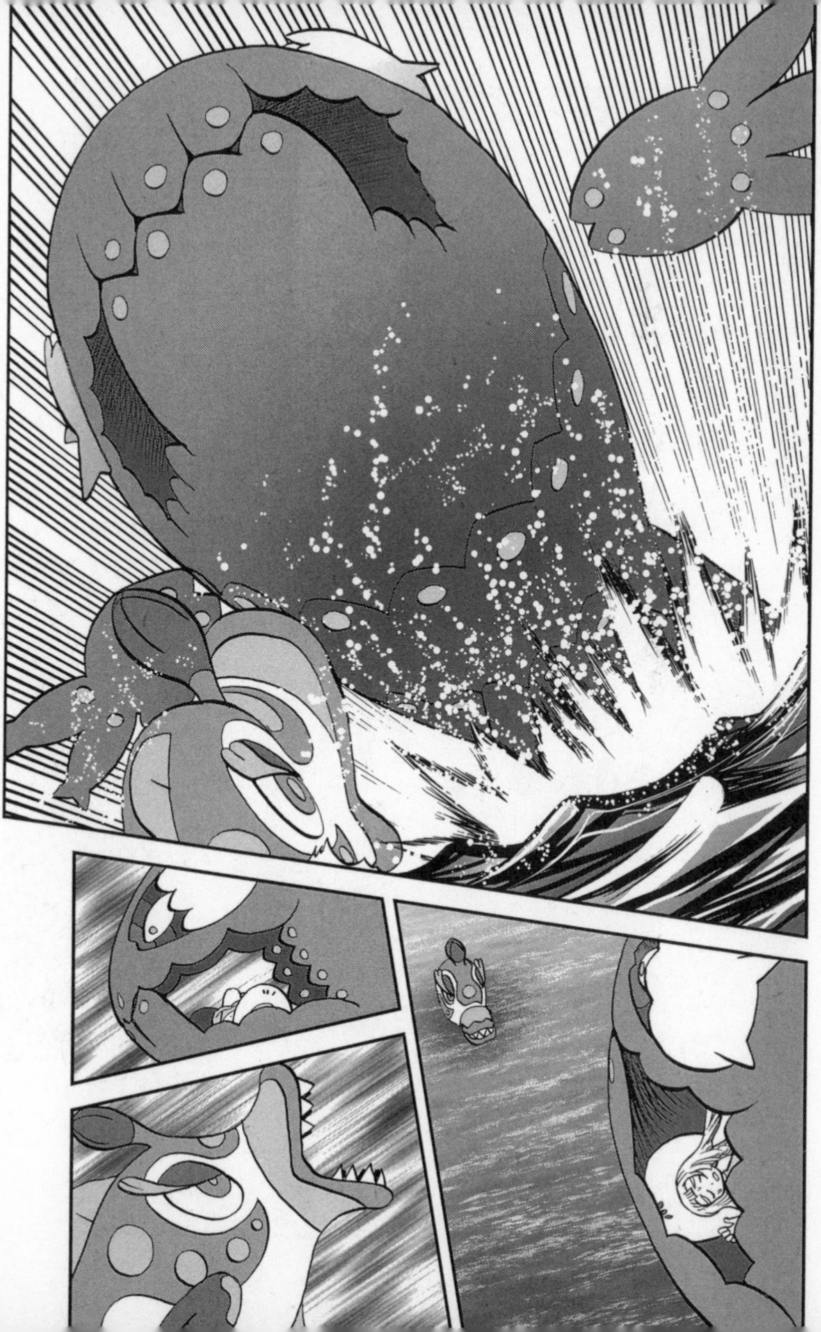

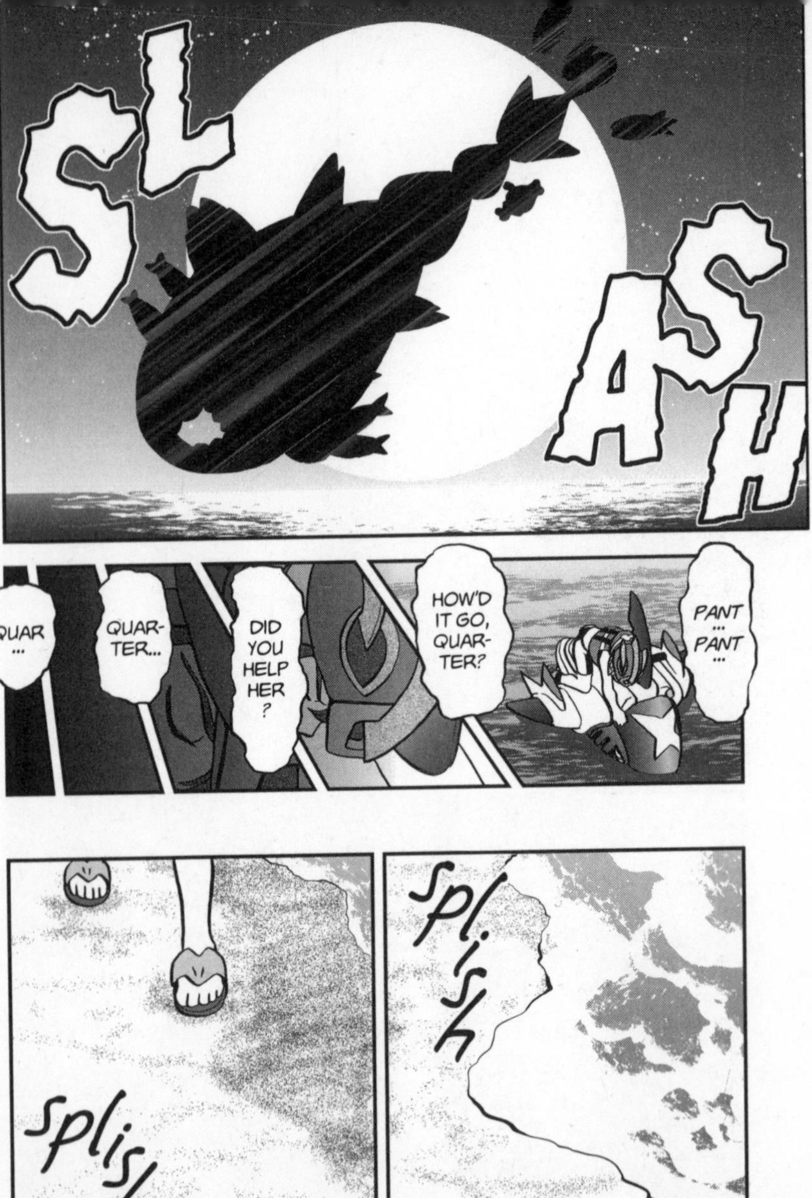
SLASH
PANT... PANT...
HOW'D IT GO, QUARTER?
DID YOU HELP HER?
QUARTER...
QUAR...
splish
splish

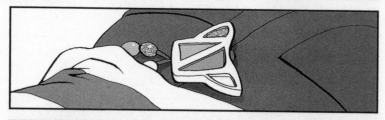

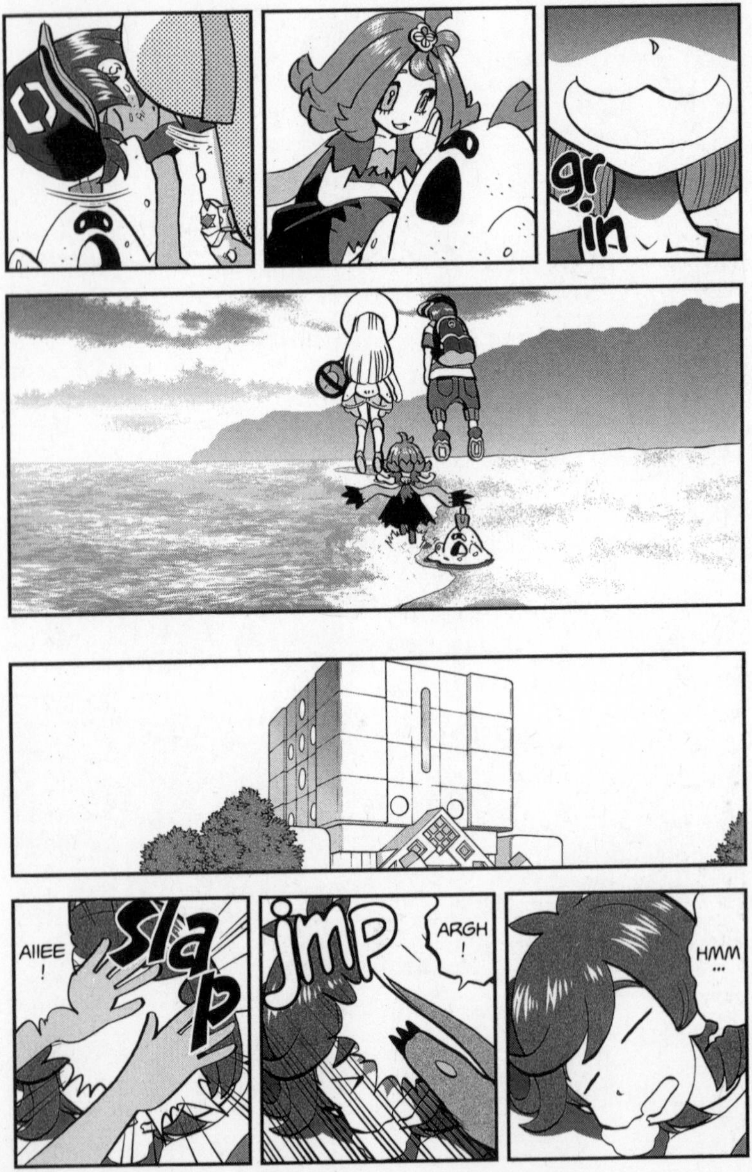

grin
HMM...
ARGH!
jmp
slap
AIIEE!

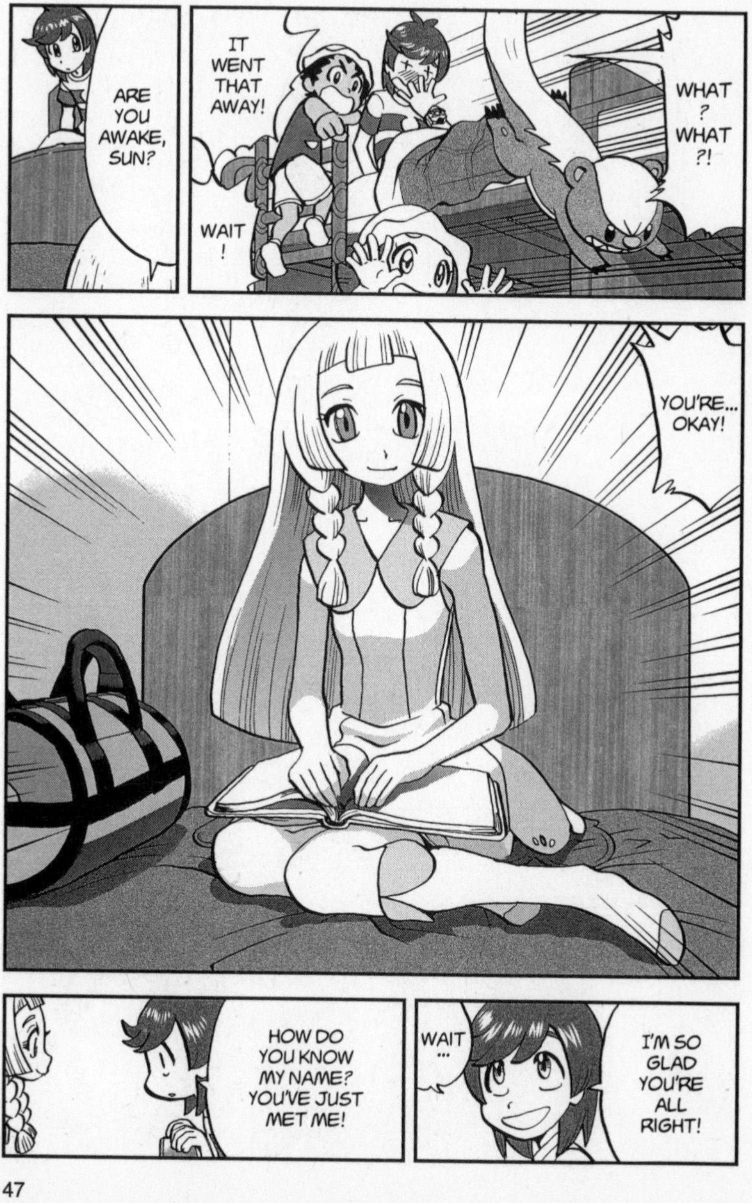

WHAT? WHAT?!
IT WENT THAT AWAY!
WAIT!
ARE YOU AWAKE, SUN?
YOU'RE... OKAY!
I'M SO GLAD YOU'RE ALL RIGHT!
WAIT...
HOW DO YOU KNOW MY NAME? YOU'VE JUST MET ME!

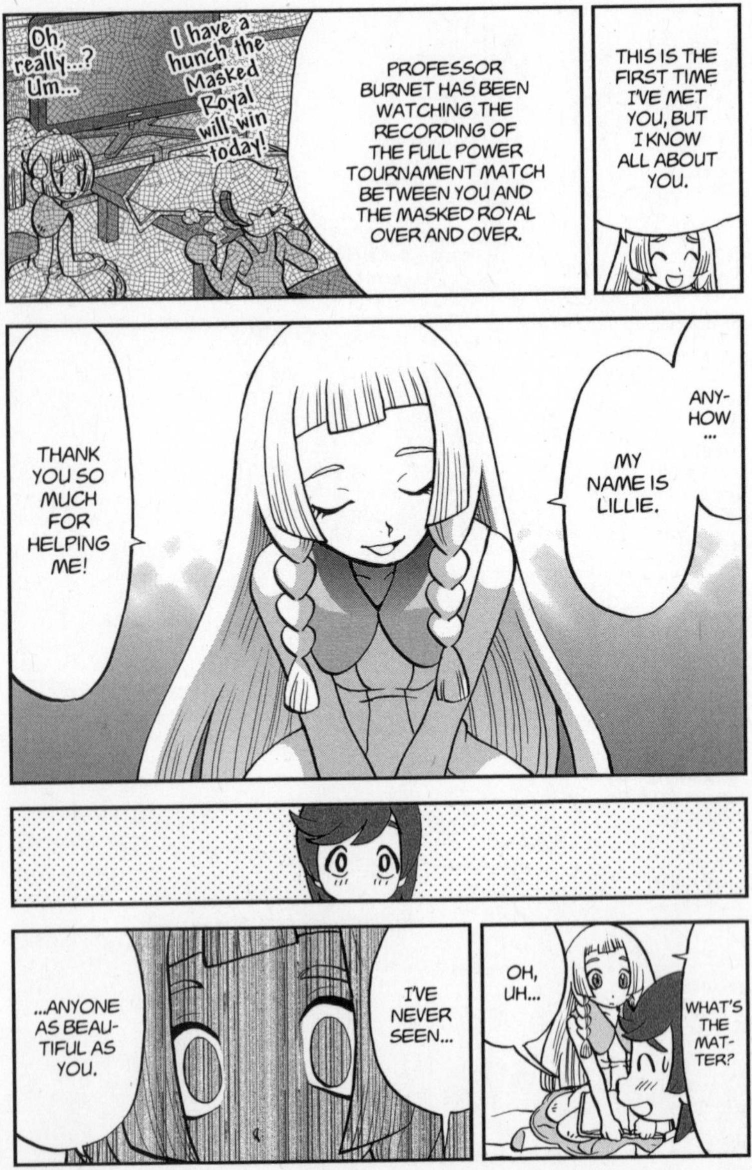
THIS IS THE FIRST TIME I'VE MET YOU, BUT I KNOW ALL ABOUT YOU.
PROFESSOR BURNET HAS BEEN WATCHING THE RECORDING OF THE FULL POWER TOURNAMENT MATCH BETWEEN YOU AND THE MASKED ROYAL OVER AND OVER.
I have a hunch the Masked Royal will win today!
Oh, really...? Um...
ANY-HOW...
MY NAME IS LILLIE.
THANK YOU SO MUCH FOR HELPING ME!
WHAT'S THE MAT-TER?
OH, UH...
I'VE NEVER SEEN...
...ANYONE AS BEAU-TIFUL AS YOU.

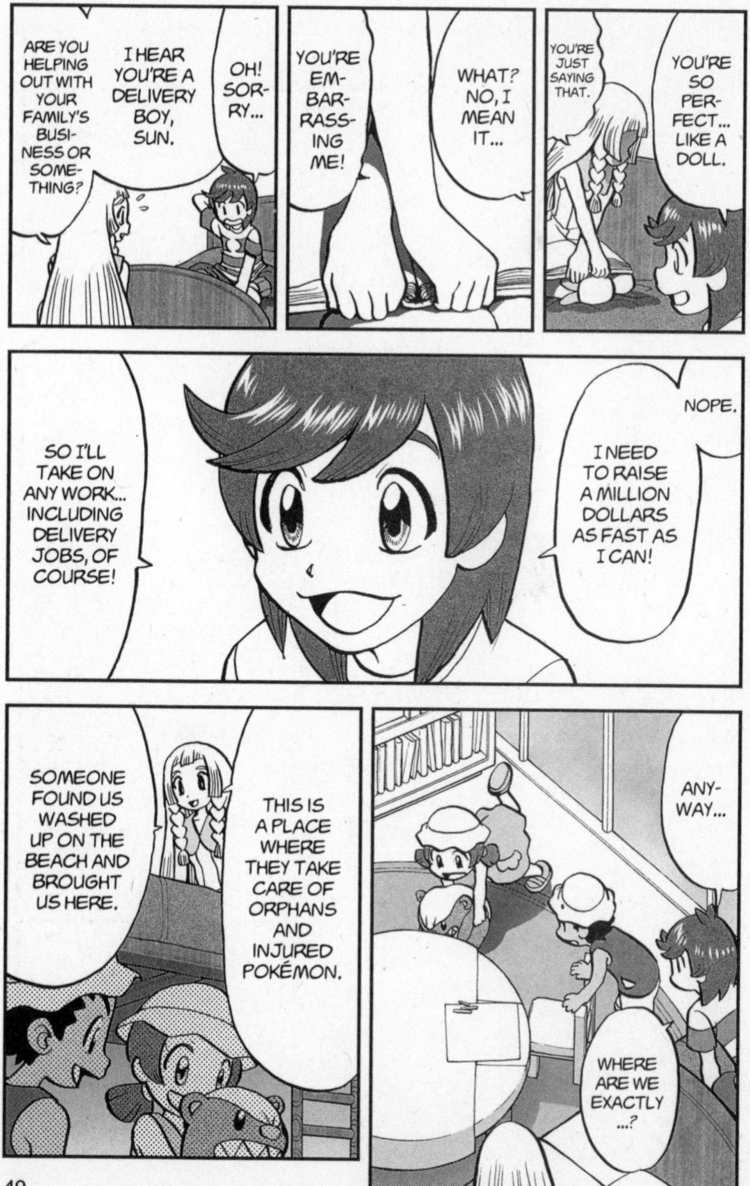
YOU'RE SO PER-FECT... LIKE A DOLL.
YOU'RE JUST SAYING THAT.
WHAT? NO, I MEAN IT...
YOU'RE EM-BAR-RASS-ING ME!
OH! SOR-RY...
I HEAR YOU'RE A DELIVERY BOY, SUN.
ARE YOU HELPING OUT WITH YOUR FAMILY'S BUSI-NESS OR SOME-THING?
NOPE.
I NEED TO RAISE A MILLION DOLLARS AS FAST AS I CAN!
SO I'LL TAKE ON ANY WORK... INCLUDING DELIVERY JOBS, OF COURSE!
ANY-WAY...
WHERE ARE WE EXACTLY ...?
THIS IS A PLACE WHERE THEY TAKE CARE OF ORPHANS AND INJURED POKÉMON.
SOMEONE FOUND US WASHED UP ON THE BEACH AND BROUGHT US HERE.

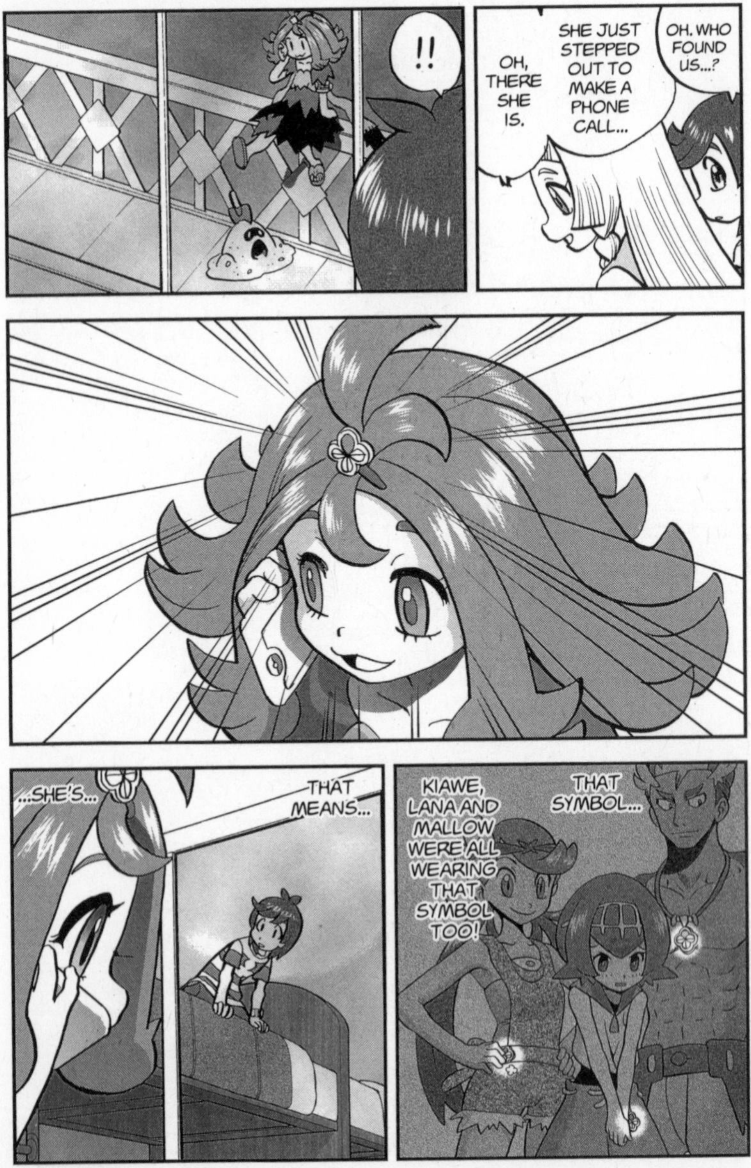
OH. WHO FOUND US...?
SHE JUST STEPPED OUT TO MAKE A PHONE CALL...
OH, THERE SHE IS.
!!
THAT SYMBOL...
KIAWE, LANA AND MALLOW WERE ALL WEARING THAT SYMBOL TOO!
THAT MEANS...
...SHE'S...

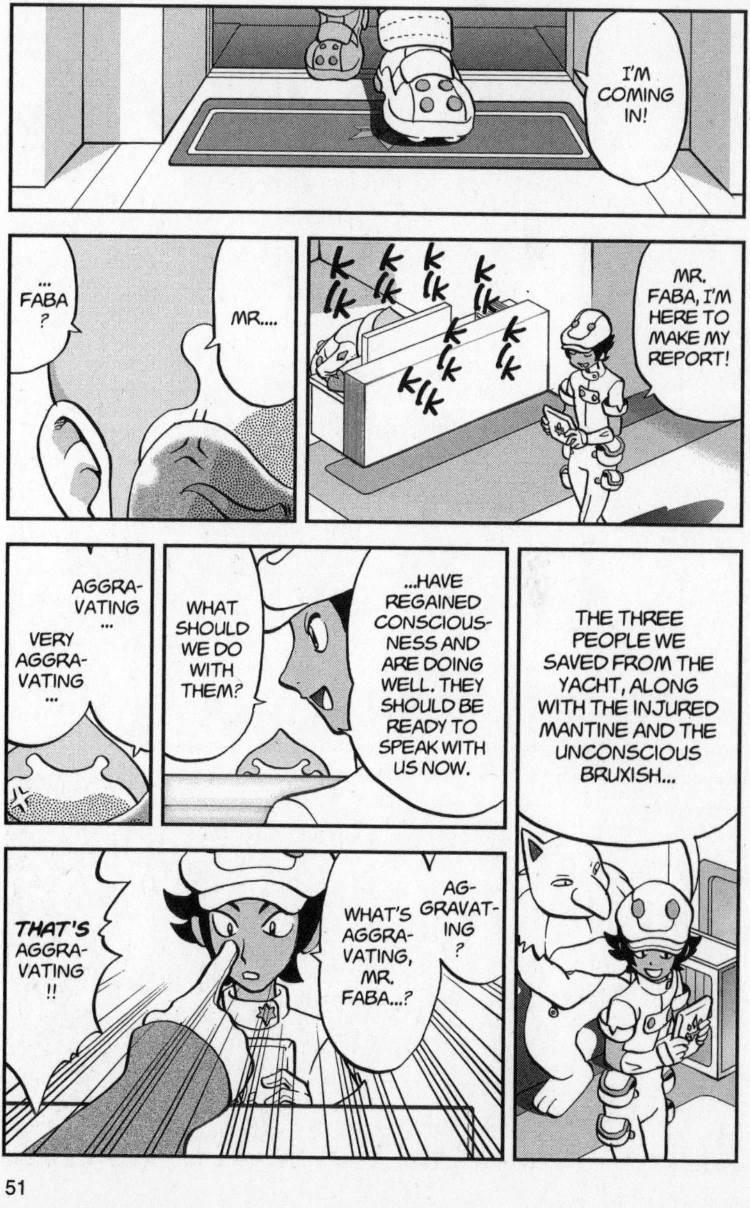
I'M COMING IN!
MR. FABA, I'M HERE TO MAKE MY REPORT!
KIK KIK KIK KIK KIK KIK KIK
MR....
... FABA?
THE THREE PEOPLE WE SAVED FROM THE YACHT, ALONG WITH THE INJURED MANTINE AND THE UNCONSCIOUS BRUXISH...
...HAVE REGAINED CONSCIOUS-NESS AND ARE DOING WELL. THEY SHOULD BE READY TO SPEAK WITH US NOW.
WHAT SHOULD WE DO WITH THEM?
AGGRA-VATING ...
VERY AGGRA-VATING ...
AG-GRAVAT-ING ?
WHAT'S AGGRA-VATING, MR. FABA...?
THAT'S AGGRA-VATING !!

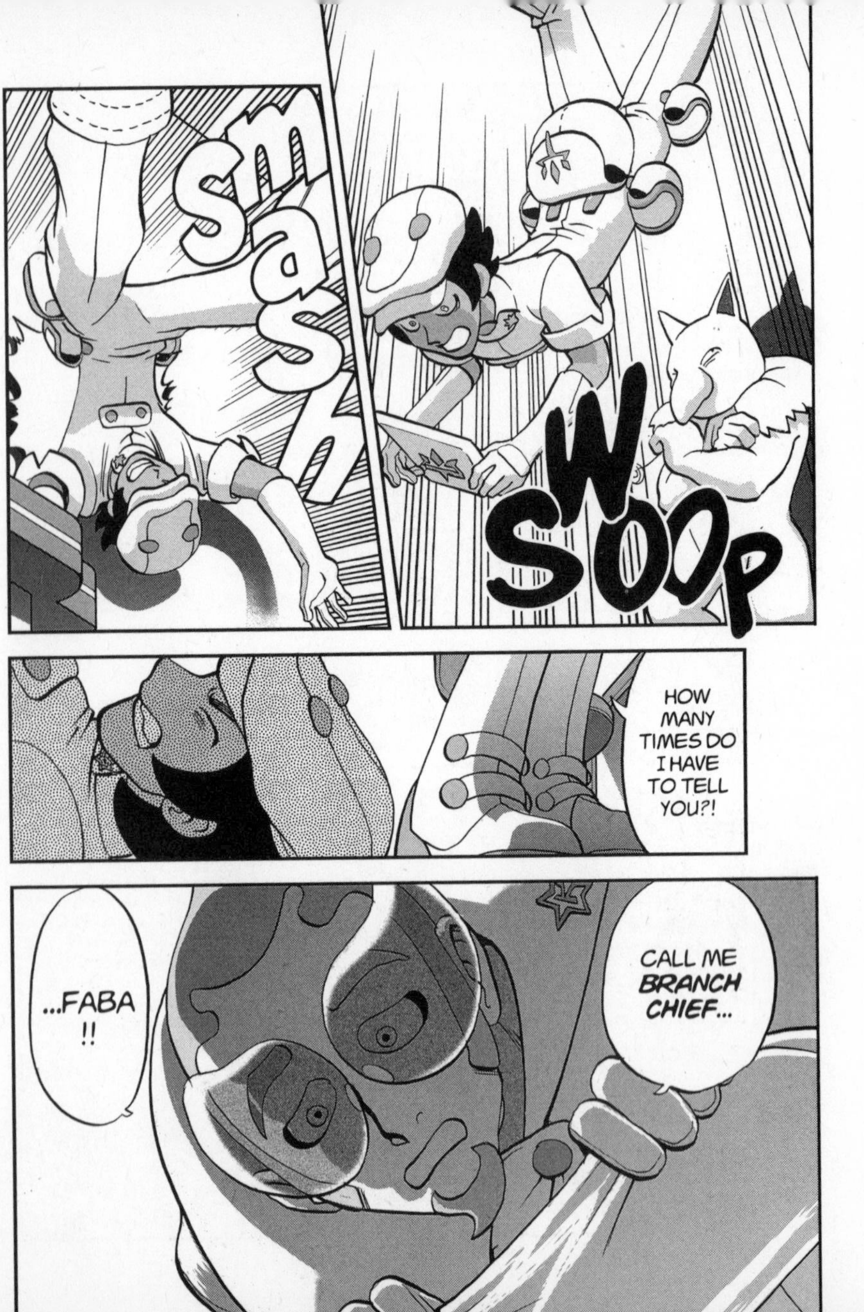
SWOOP
SMASH
HOW MANY TIMES DO I HAVE TO TELL YOU?!
CALL ME *BRANCH CHIEF*...
...FABA !!

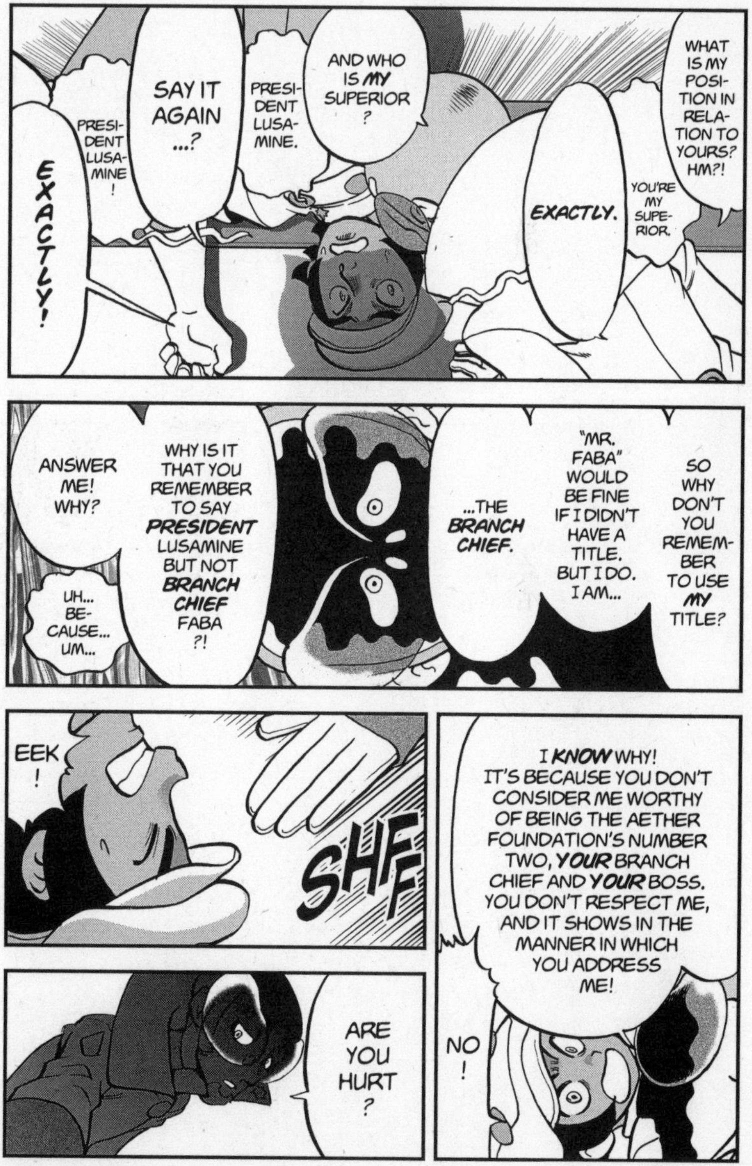
WHAT IS MY POSITION IN RELATION TO YOURS? HM?!
YOU'RE MY SUPERIOR.
EXACTLY.
AND WHO IS MY SUPERIOR?
PRESIDENT LUSAMINE.
SAY IT AGAIN...?
PRESIDENT LUSAMINE!
EXACTLY!
SO WHY DON'T YOU REMEMBER TO USE MY TITLE?
"MR. FABA" WOULD BE FINE IF I DIDN'T HAVE A TITLE. BUT I DO. I AM...
...THE BRANCH CHIEF.
WHY IS IT THAT YOU REMEMBER TO SAY PRESIDENT LUSAMINE BUT NOT BRANCH CHIEF FABA?!
ANSWER ME! WHY?
UH... BECAUSE... UM...
I KNOW WHY! IT'S BECAUSE YOU DON'T CONSIDER ME WORTHY OF BEING THE AETHER FOUNDATION'S NUMBER TWO, YOUR BRANCH CHIEF AND YOUR BOSS. YOU DON'T RESPECT ME, AND IT SHOWS IN THE MANNER IN WHICH YOU ADDRESS ME!
NO!
EEK!
SHFF
ARE YOU HURT?

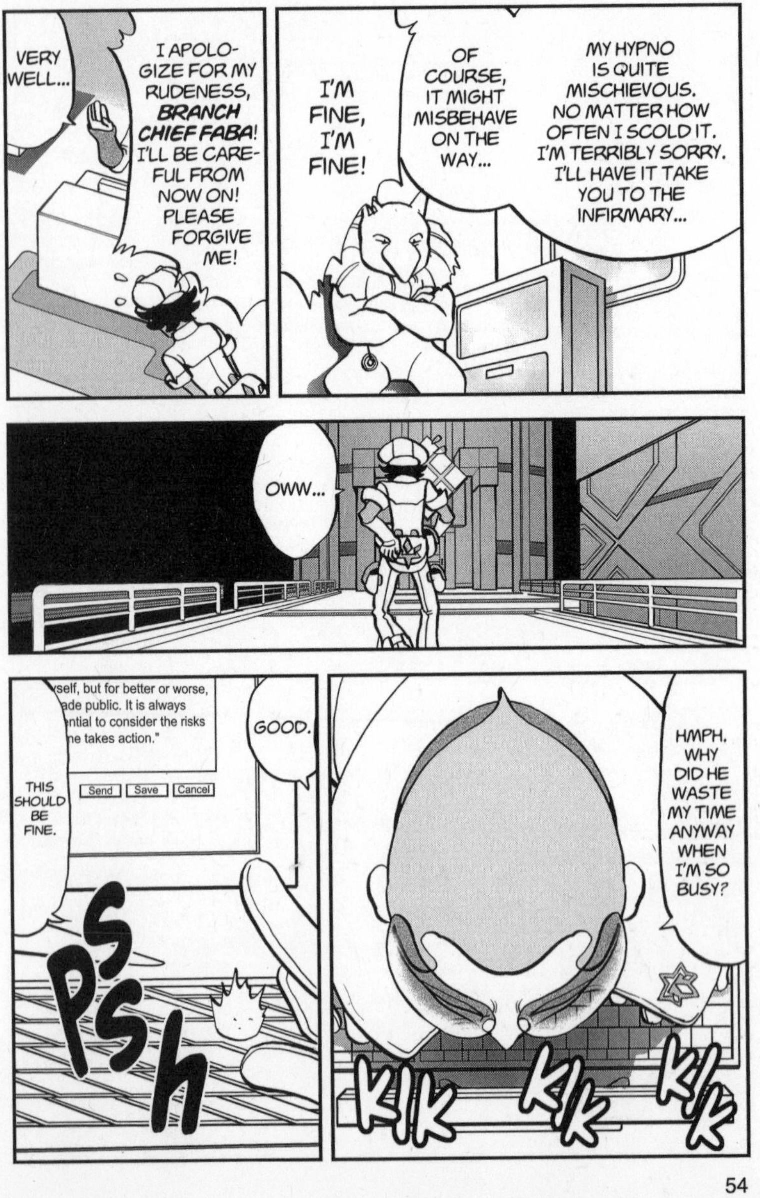
MY HYPNO IS QUITE MISCHIEVOUS. NO MATTER HOW OFTEN I SCOLD IT. I'M TERRIBLY SORRY. I'LL HAVE IT TAKE YOU TO THE INFIRMARY...
OF COURSE, IT MIGHT MISBEHAVE ON THE WAY...
I'M FINE, I'M FINE!
I APOLOGIZE FOR MY RUDENESS, **BRANCH CHIEF FABA**! I'LL BE CAREFUL FROM NOW ON! PLEASE FORGIVE ME!
VERY WELL...
OWW...
HMPH. WHY DID HE WASTE MY TIME ANYWAY WHEN I'M SO BUSY?
KIK KIK KIK
GOOD.
yself, but for better or worse,
ade public. It is always
ential to consider the risks
ne takes action."
Send Save Cancel
THIS SHOULD BE FINE.
PSSH

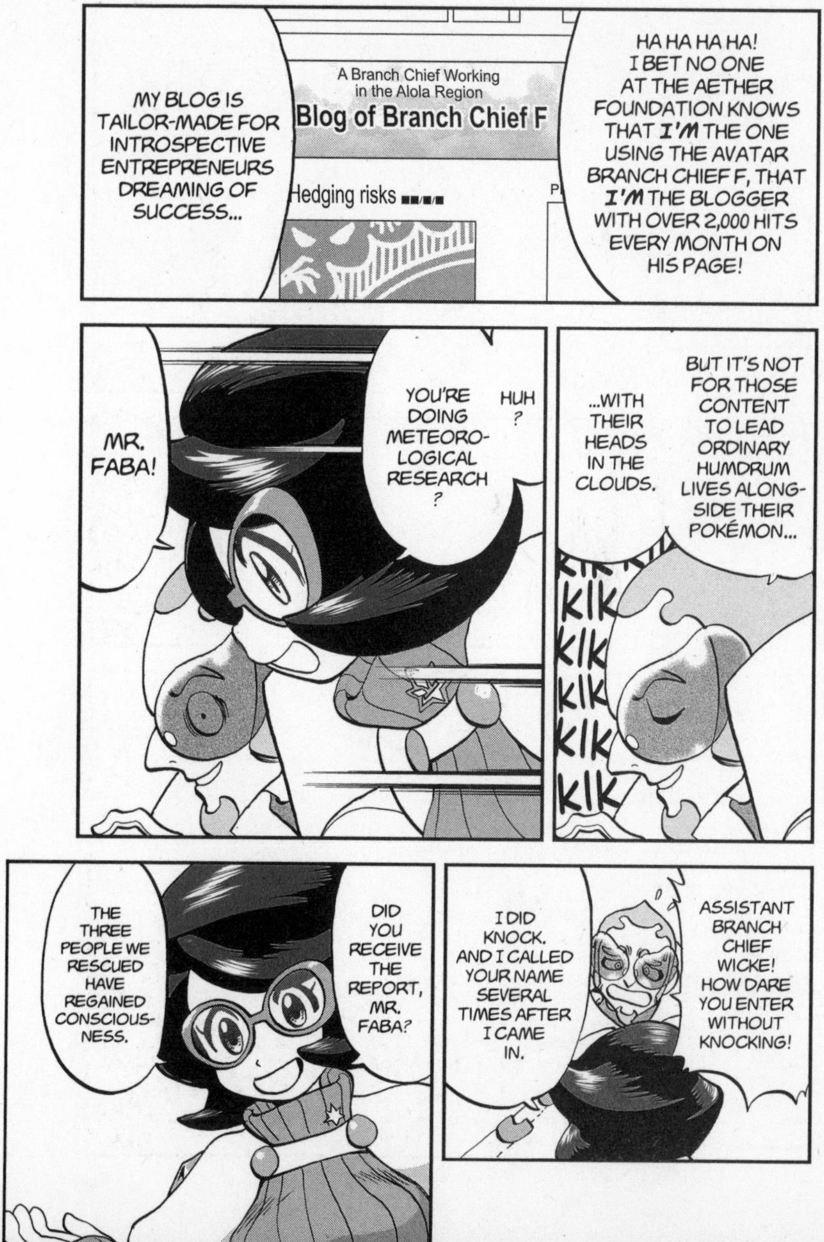
HA HA HA HA! I BET NO ONE AT THE AETHER FOUNDATION KNOWS THAT ***I'M*** THE ONE USING THE AVATAR BRANCH CHIEF F, THAT ***I'M*** THE BLOGGER WITH OVER 2,000 HITS EVERY MONTH ON HIS PAGE!
A Branch Chief Working in the Alola Region
Blog of Branch Chief F
Hedging risks
MY BLOG IS TAILOR-MADE FOR INTROSPECTIVE ENTREPRENEURS DREAMING OF SUCCESS...
BUT IT'S NOT FOR THOSE CONTENT TO LEAD ORDINARY HUMDRUM LIVES ALONGSIDE THEIR POKÉMON...
...WITH THEIR HEADS IN THE CLOUDS.
KIK KIK KIK KIK KIK KIK
HUH?
YOU'RE DOING METEOROLOGICAL RESEARCH?
MR. FABA!
ASSISTANT BRANCH CHIEF WICKE! HOW DARE YOU ENTER WITHOUT KNOCKING!
I DID KNOCK. AND I CALLED YOUR NAME SEVERAL TIMES AFTER I CAME IN.
DID YOU RECEIVE THE REPORT, MR. FABA?
THE THREE PEOPLE WE RESCUED HAVE REGAINED CONSCIOUSNESS.

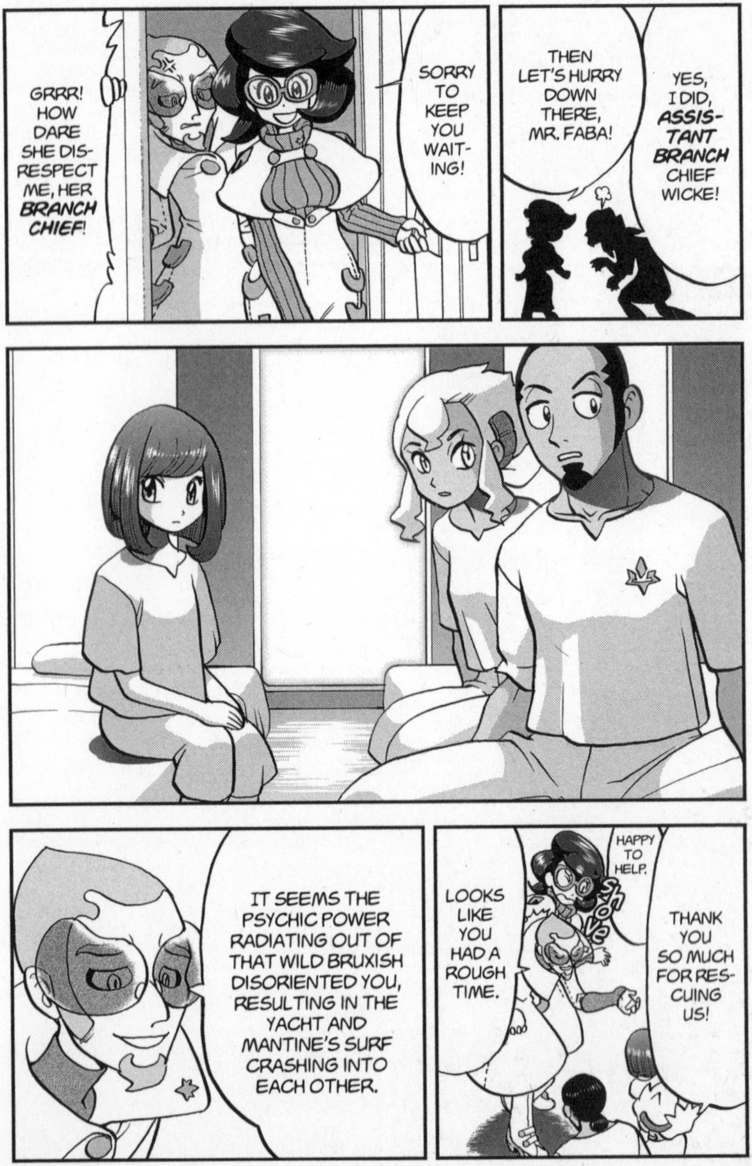
YES, I DID, ASSISTANT BRANCH CHIEF WICKE!
THEN LET'S HURRY DOWN THERE, MR. FABA!
SORRY TO KEEP YOU WAITING!
GRRR! HOW DARE SHE DISRESPECT ME, HER BRANCH CHIEF!
THANK YOU SO MUCH FOR RESCUING US!
HAPPY TO HELP.
SHOVE
LOOKS LIKE YOU HAD A ROUGH TIME.
IT SEEMS THE PSYCHIC POWER RADIATING OUT OF THAT WILD BRUXISH DISORIENTED YOU, RESULTING IN THE YACHT AND MANTINE'S SURF CRASHING INTO EACH OTHER.

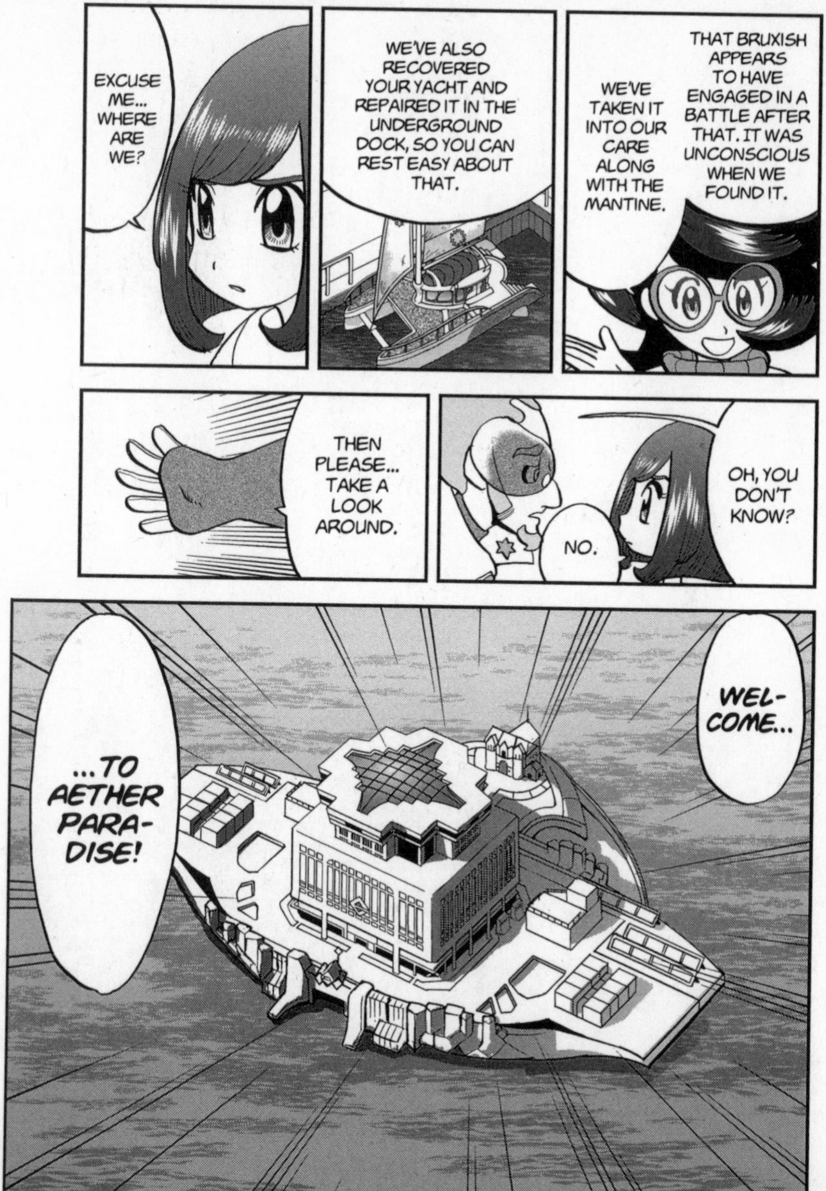
THAT BRUXISH APPEARS TO HAVE ENGAGED IN A BATTLE AFTER THAT. IT WAS UNCONSCIOUS WHEN WE FOUND IT.
WE'VE TAKEN IT INTO OUR CARE ALONG WITH THE MANTINE.
WE'VE ALSO RECOVERED YOUR YACHT AND REPAIRED IT IN THE UNDERGROUND DOCK, SO YOU CAN REST EASY ABOUT THAT.
EXCUSE ME... WHERE ARE WE?
OH, YOU DON'T KNOW?
NO.
THEN PLEASE... TAKE A LOOK AROUND.
WEL-COME...
...TO AETHER PARA-DISE!

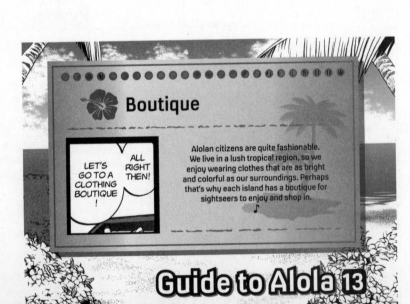

Guide to Alola 13

Boutique

ALL RIGHT THEN!
LET'S GO TO A CLOTHING BOUTIQUE!

Alolan citizens are quite fashionable. We live in a lush tropical region, so we enjoy wearing clothes that are as bright and colorful as our surroundings. Perhaps that's why each island has a boutique for sightseers to enjoy and shop in. ♪

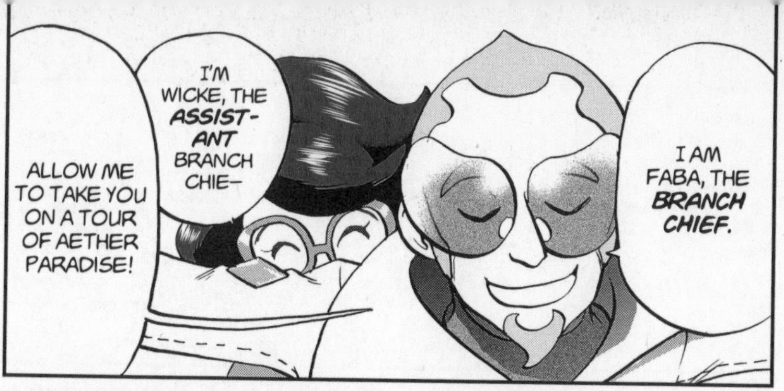
I AM FABA, THE BRANCH CHIEF.
I'M WICKE, THE ASSISTANT BRANCH CHIE–
ALLOW ME TO TAKE YOU ON A TOUR OF AETHER PARADISE!

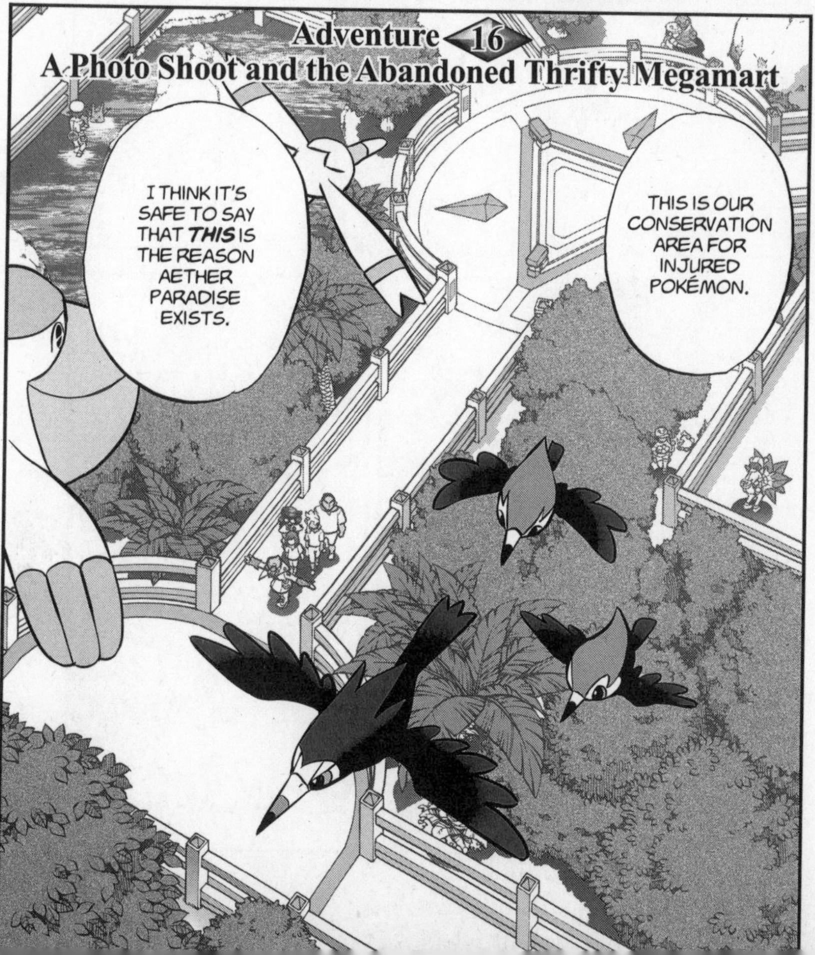
Adventure 16
A Photo Shoot and the Abandoned Thrifty Megamart
THIS IS OUR CONSERVATION AREA FOR INJURED POKÉMON.
I THINK IT'S SAFE TO SAY THAT THIS IS THE REASON AETHER PARADISE EXISTS.

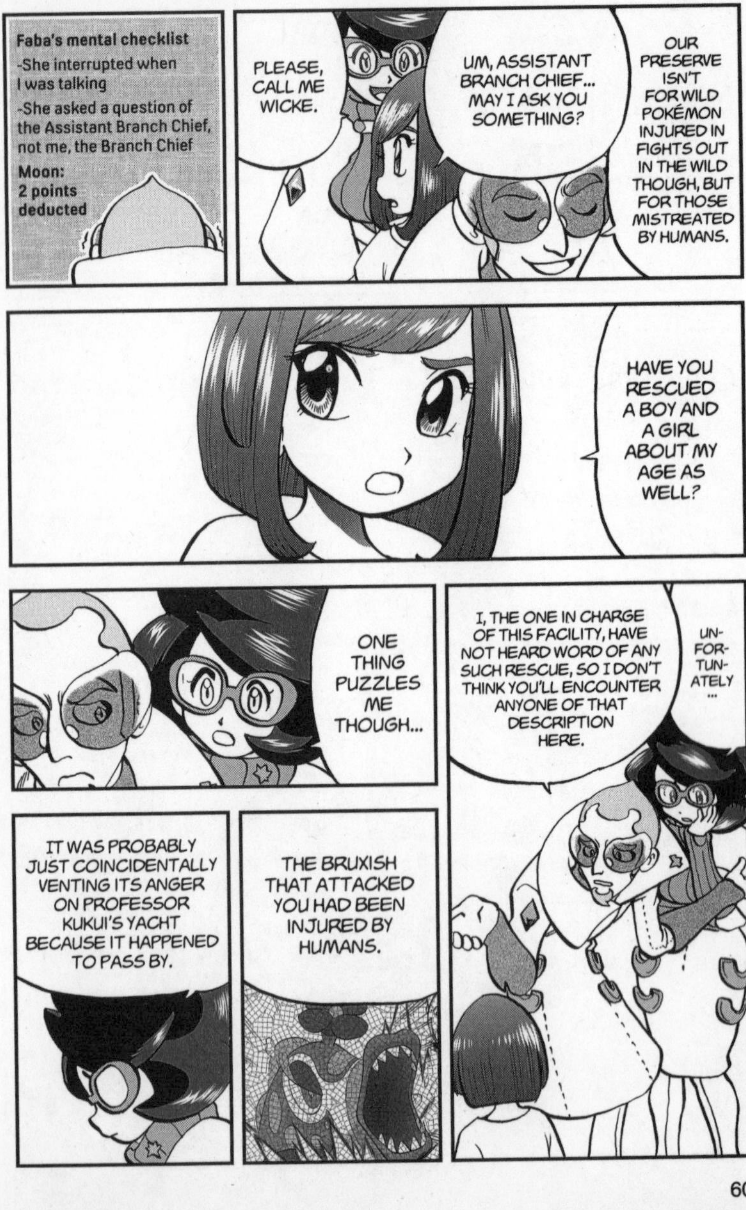
OUR PRESERVE ISN'T FOR WILD POKéMON INJURED IN FIGHTS OUT IN THE WILD THOUGH, BUT FOR THOSE MISTREATED BY HUMANS.
UM, ASSISTANT BRANCH CHIEF... MAY I ASK YOU SOMETHING?
PLEASE, CALL ME WICKE.
Faba's mental checklist
-She interrupted when I was talking
-She asked a question of the Assistant Branch Chief, not me, the Branch Chief
Moon: 2 points deducted
HAVE YOU RESCUED A BOY AND A GIRL ABOUT MY AGE AS WELL?
UN-FOR-TUN-ATELY...
I, THE ONE IN CHARGE OF THIS FACILITY, HAVE NOT HEARD WORD OF ANY SUCH RESCUE, SO I DON'T THINK YOU'LL ENCOUNTER ANYONE OF THAT DESCRIPTION HERE.
ONE THING PUZZLES ME THOUGH...
THE BRUXISH THAT ATTACKED YOU HAD BEEN INJURED BY HUMANS.
IT WAS PROBABLY JUST COINCIDENTALLY VENTING ITS ANGER ON PROFESSOR KUKUI'S YACHT BECAUSE IT HAPPENED TO PASS BY.

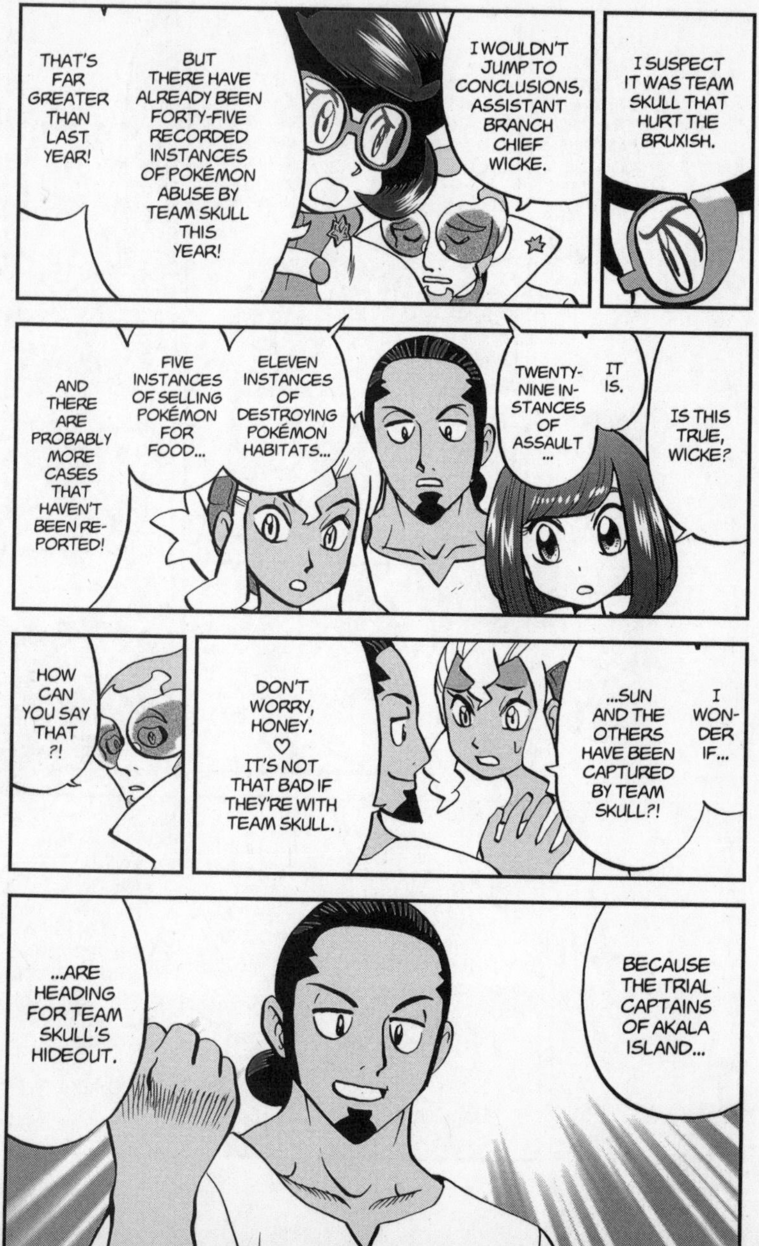
I SUSPECT IT WAS TEAM SKULL THAT HURT THE BRUXISH.
I WOULDN'T JUMP TO CONCLUSIONS, ASSISTANT BRANCH CHIEF WICKE.
BUT THERE HAVE ALREADY BEEN FORTY-FIVE RECORDED INSTANCES OF POKÉMON ABUSE BY TEAM SKULL THIS YEAR!
THAT'S FAR GREATER THAN LAST YEAR!
IS THIS TRUE, WICKE?
IT IS.
TWENTY-NINE INSTANCES OF ASSAULT...
ELEVEN INSTANCES OF DESTROYING POKÉMON HABITATS...
FIVE INSTANCES OF SELLING POKÉMON FOR FOOD...
AND THERE ARE PROBABLY MORE CASES THAT HAVEN'T BEEN REPORTED!
I WONDER IF...
...SUN AND THE OTHERS HAVE BEEN CAPTURED BY TEAM SKULL?!
DON'T WORRY, HONEY. ♡ IT'S NOT THAT BAD IF THEY'RE WITH TEAM SKULL.
HOW CAN YOU SAY THAT?!
BECAUSE THE TRIAL CAPTAINS OF AKALA ISLAND...
...ARE HEADING FOR TEAM SKULL'S HIDEOUT.

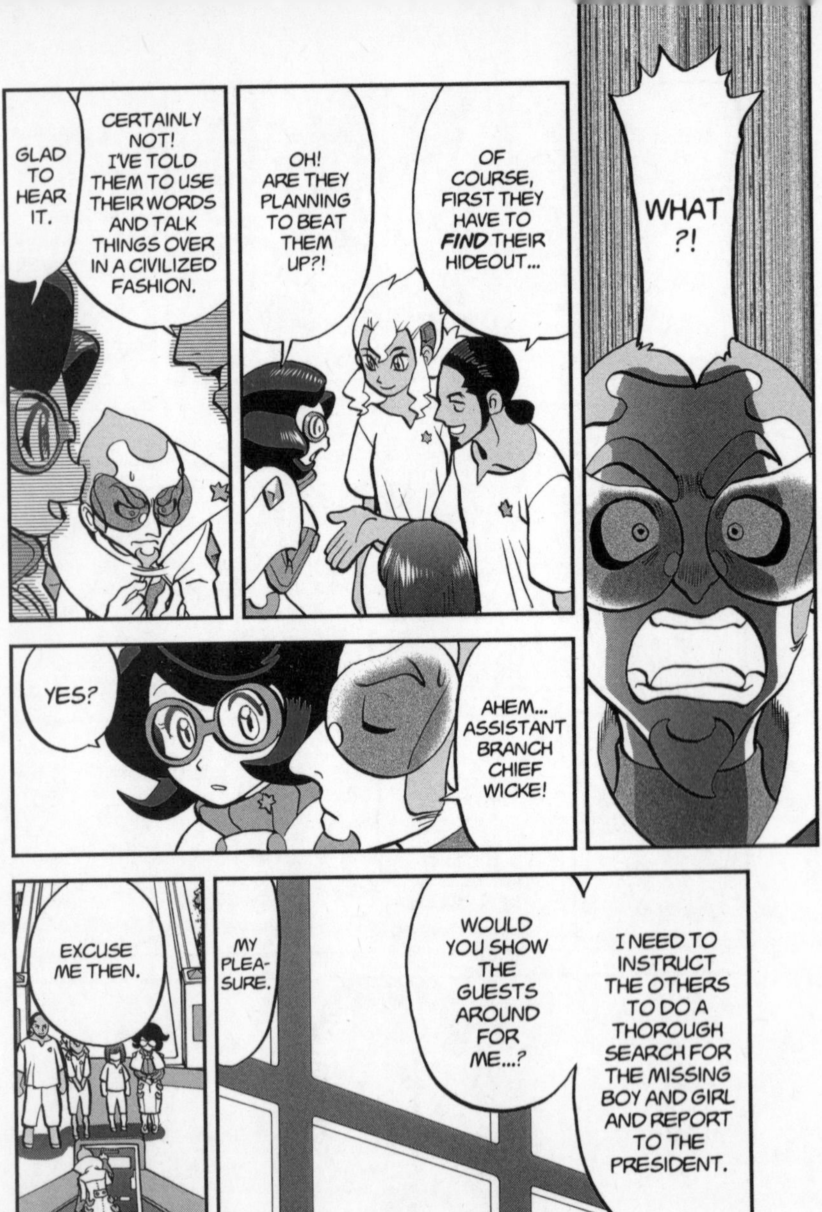
WHAT ?!
OF COURSE, FIRST THEY HAVE TO *FIND* THEIR HIDEOUT...
OH! ARE THEY PLANNING TO BEAT THEM UP?!
CERTAINLY NOT! I'VE TOLD THEM TO USE THEIR WORDS AND TALK THINGS OVER IN A CIVILIZED FASHION.
GLAD TO HEAR IT.
AHEM... ASSISTANT BRANCH CHIEF WICKE!
YES?
I NEED TO INSTRUCT THE OTHERS TO DO A THOROUGH SEARCH FOR THE MISSING BOY AND GIRL AND REPORT TO THE PRESIDENT.
WOULD YOU SHOW THE GUESTS AROUND FOR ME...?
MY PLEA-SURE.
EXCUSE ME THEN.

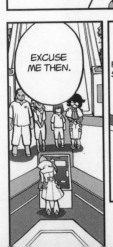

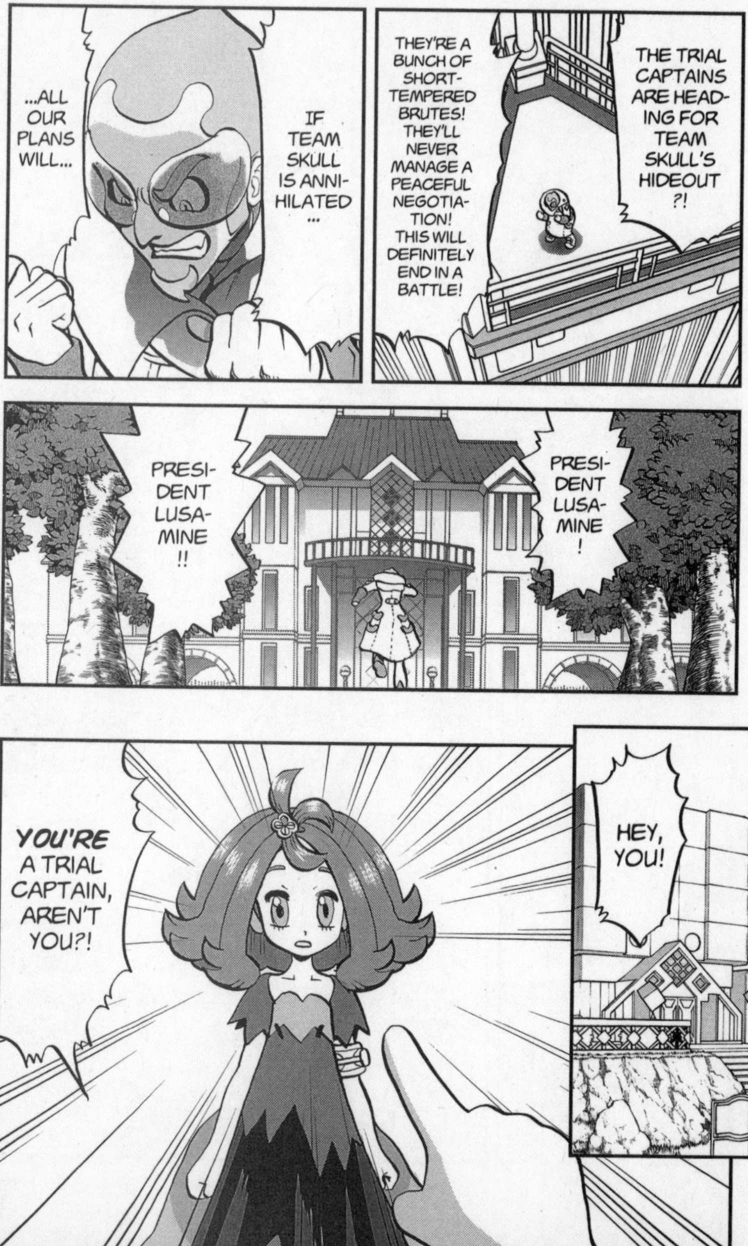
THE TRIAL CAPTAINS ARE HEADING FOR TEAM SKULL'S HIDEOUT ?!
THEY'RE A BUNCH OF SHORT-TEMPERED BRUTES! THEY'LL NEVER MANAGE A PEACEFUL NEGOTIATION! THIS WILL DEFINITELY END IN A BATTLE!
IF TEAM SKULL IS ANNIHILATED ...
...ALL OUR PLANS WILL...
PRESIDENT LUSAMINE !
PRESIDENT LUSAMINE !!
HEY, YOU!
YOU'RE A TRIAL CAPTAIN, AREN'T YOU?!

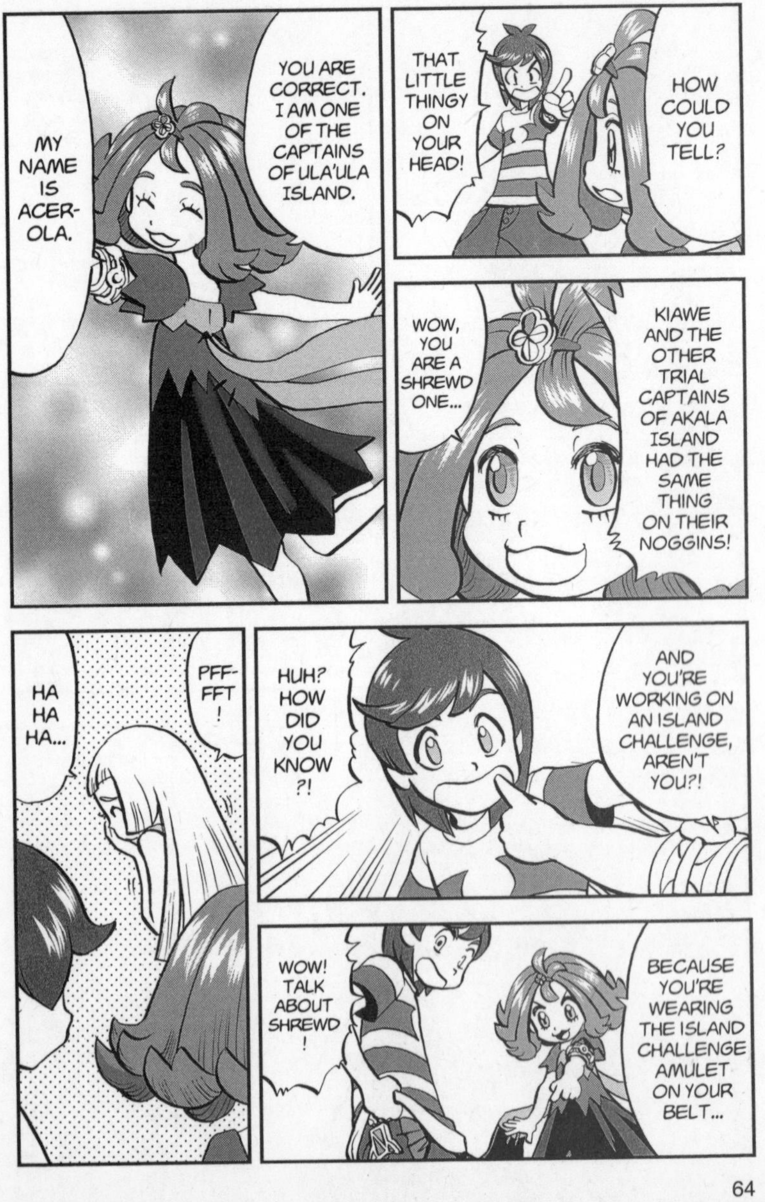
HOW COULD YOU TELL?
THAT LITTLE THINGY ON YOUR HEAD!
KIAWE AND THE OTHER TRIAL CAPTAINS OF AKALA ISLAND HAD THE SAME THING ON THEIR NOGGINS!
WOW, YOU ARE A SHREWD ONE...
YOU ARE CORRECT. I AM ONE OF THE CAPTAINS OF ULA'ULA ISLAND.
MY NAME IS ACER-OLA.
AND YOU'RE WORKING ON AN ISLAND CHALLENGE, AREN'T YOU?!
HUH? HOW DID YOU KNOW ?!
BECAUSE YOU'RE WEARING THE ISLAND CHALLENGE AMULET ON YOUR BELT...
WOW! TALK ABOUT SHREWD !
PFF-FFT !
HA HA HA...

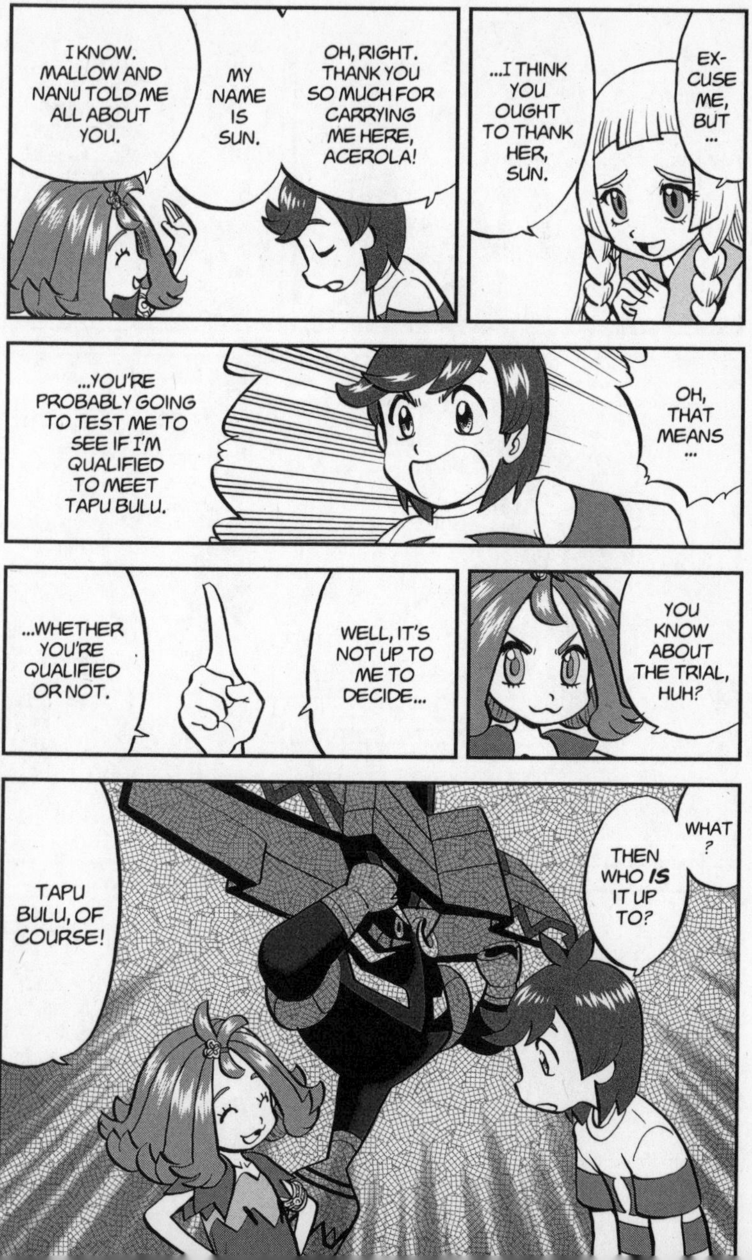
EX-CUSE ME, BUT ...
...I THINK YOU OUGHT TO THANK HER, SUN.
OH, RIGHT. THANK YOU SO MUCH FOR CARRYING ME HERE, ACEROLA!
MY NAME IS SUN.
I KNOW. MALLOW AND NANU TOLD ME ALL ABOUT YOU.
OH, THAT MEANS ...
...YOU'RE PROBABLY GOING TO TEST ME TO SEE IF I'M QUALIFIED TO MEET TAPU BULU.
YOU KNOW ABOUT THE TRIAL, HUH?
WELL, IT'S NOT UP TO ME TO DECIDE...
...WHETHER YOU'RE QUALIFIED OR NOT.
WHAT?
THEN WHO **IS** IT UP TO?
TAPU BULU, OF COURSE!

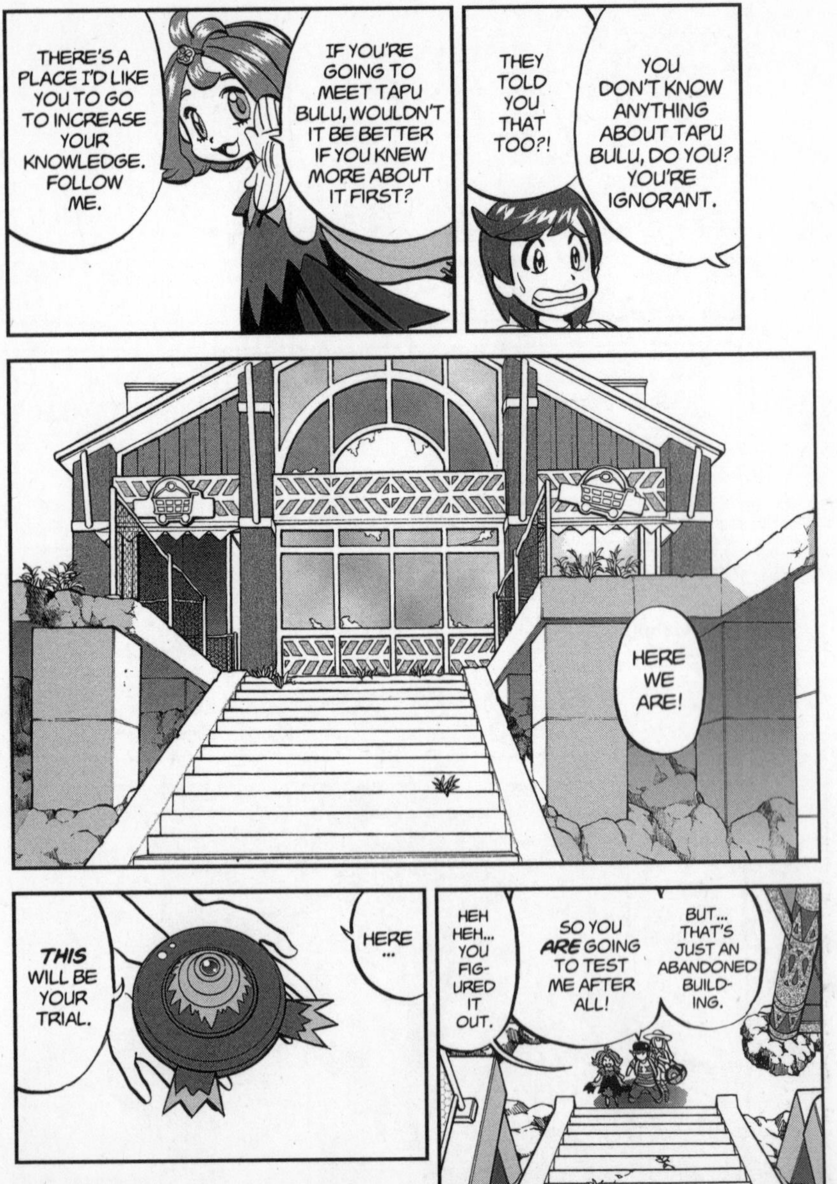
YOU DON'T KNOW ANYTHING ABOUT TAPU BULU, DO YOU? YOU'RE IGNORANT.
THEY TOLD YOU THAT TOO?!
IF YOU'RE GOING TO MEET TAPU BULU, WOULDN'T IT BE BETTER IF YOU KNEW MORE ABOUT IT FIRST?
THERE'S A PLACE I'D LIKE YOU TO GO TO INCREASE YOUR KNOWLEDGE. FOLLOW ME.
HERE WE ARE!
BUT... THAT'S JUST AN ABANDONED BUILD-ING.
SO YOU **ARE** GOING TO TEST ME AFTER ALL!
HEH HEH... YOU FIG-URED IT OUT.
HERE...
THIS WILL BE YOUR TRIAL.

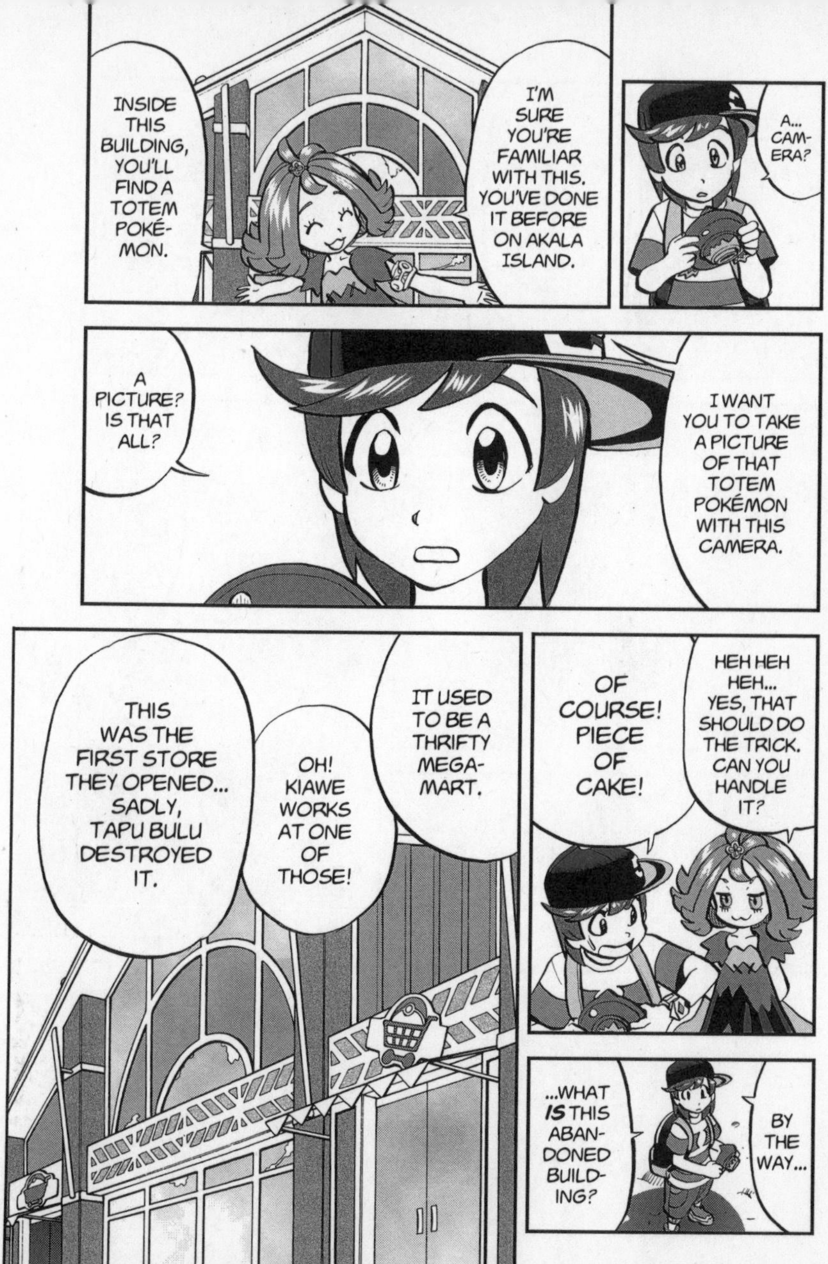
A... CAM-ERA?
I'M SURE YOU'RE FAMILIAR WITH THIS. YOU'VE DONE IT BEFORE ON AKALA ISLAND.
INSIDE THIS BUILDING, YOU'LL FIND A TOTEM POKÉ-MON.
I WANT YOU TO TAKE A PICTURE OF THAT TOTEM POKÉMON WITH THIS CAMERA.
A PICTURE? IS THAT ALL?
HEH HEH HEH... YES, THAT SHOULD DO THE TRICK. CAN YOU HANDLE IT?
OF COURSE! PIECE OF CAKE!
BY THE WAY...
...WHAT ***IS*** THIS ABAN-DONED BUILD-ING?
IT USED TO BE A THRIFTY MEGA-MART.
OH! KIAWE WORKS AT ONE OF THOSE!
THIS WAS THE FIRST STORE THEY OPENED... SADLY, TAPU BULU DESTROYED IT.

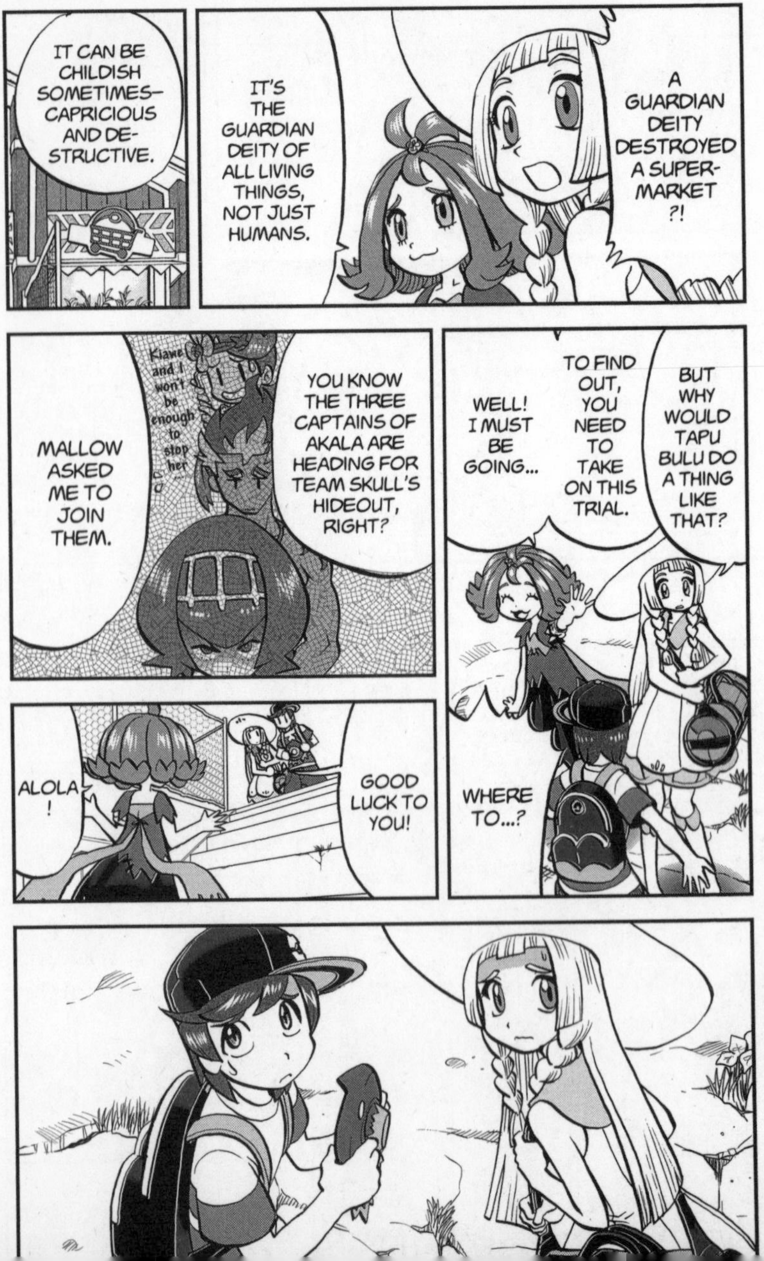
A GUARDIAN DEITY DESTROYED A SUPER-MARKET?!
IT'S THE GUARDIAN DEITY OF ALL LIVING THINGS, NOT JUST HUMANS.
IT CAN BE CHILDISH SOMETIMES—CAPRICIOUS AND DE-STRUCTIVE.
BUT WHY WOULD TAPU BULU DO A THING LIKE THAT?
TO FIND OUT, YOU NEED TO TAKE ON THIS TRIAL.
WELL! I MUST BE GOING...
WHERE TO...?
YOU KNOW THE THREE CAPTAINS OF AKALA ARE HEADING FOR TEAM SKULL'S HIDEOUT, RIGHT?
Kiawe and I won't be enough to stop her...
MALLOW ASKED ME TO JOIN THEM.
GOOD LUCK TO YOU!
ALOLA!

SKWEEEEEK

WELL...

LET'S GO IN!

ALL RIGHT.

WHOOOOSH

GLOOOOOOOM

EEK!!

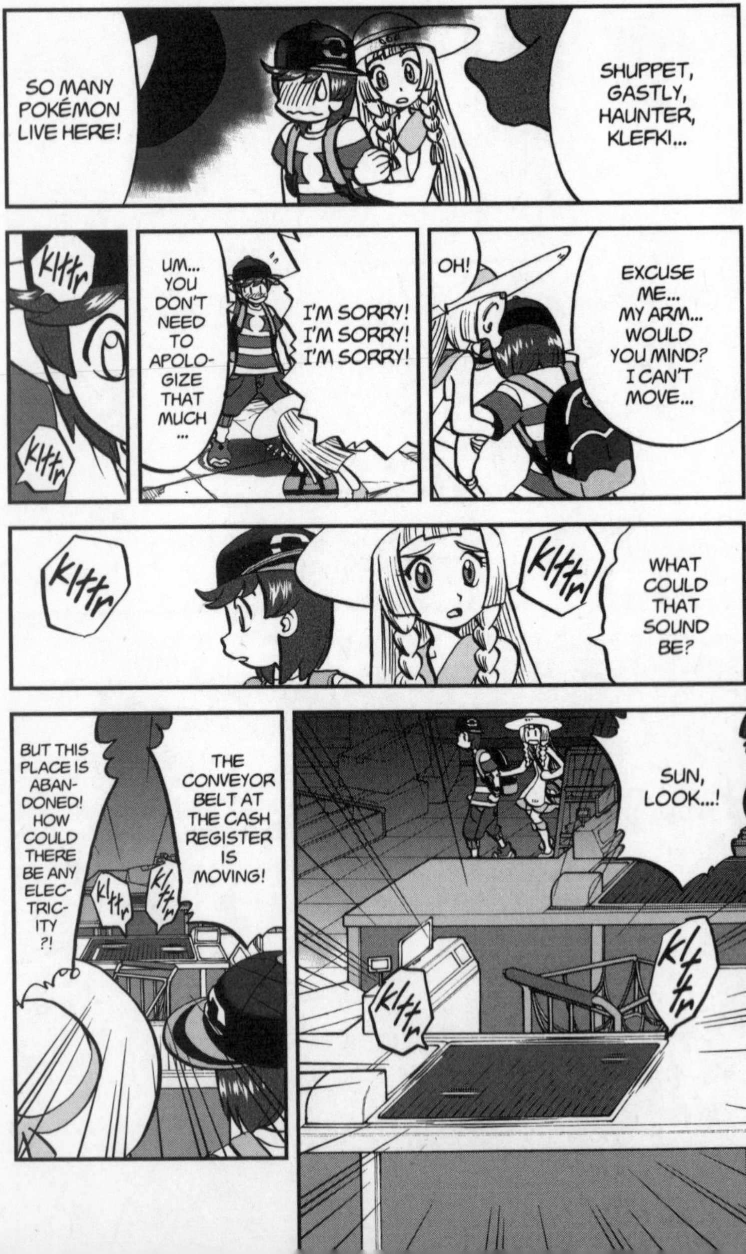
SHUPPET, GASTLY, HAUNTER, KLEFKI...
SO MANY POKÉMON LIVE HERE!
EXCUSE ME... MY ARM... WOULD YOU MIND? I CAN'T MOVE...
OH!
I'M SORRY! I'M SORRY! I'M SORRY!
UM... YOU DON'T NEED TO APOLOGIZE THAT MUCH...
Klttr
Klttr
WHAT COULD THAT SOUND BE?
Klttr
Klttr
SUN, LOOK...!
Klttr
Klttr
THE CONVEYOR BELT AT THE CASH REGISTER IS MOVING!
BUT THIS PLACE IS ABANDONED! HOW COULD THERE BE ANY ELECTRICITY?!
Klttr
Klttr

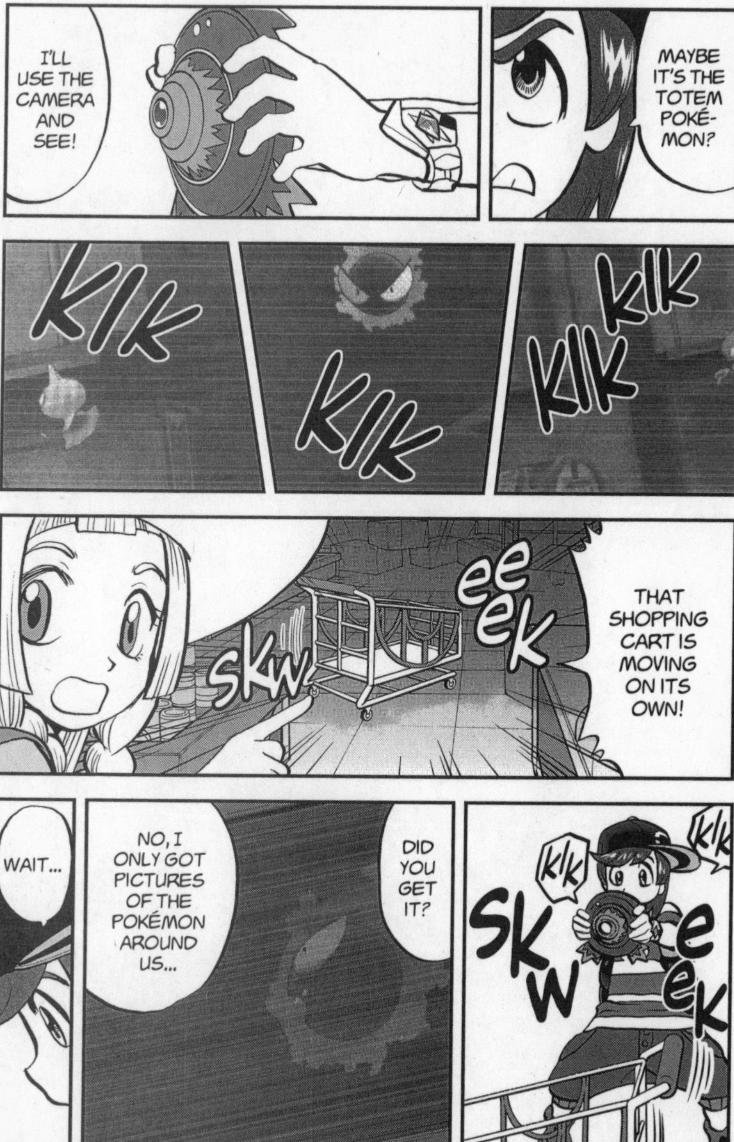
MAYBE IT'S THE TOTEM POKÉMON?
I'LL USE THE CAMERA AND SEE!
KIK
KIK
KIK
KIK
THAT SHOPPING CART IS MOVING ON ITS OWN!
eeeek
SKW
KIK
KIK
SKW
eeek
DID YOU GET IT?
NO, I ONLY GOT PICTURES OF THE POKÉMON AROUND US...
WAIT...

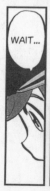

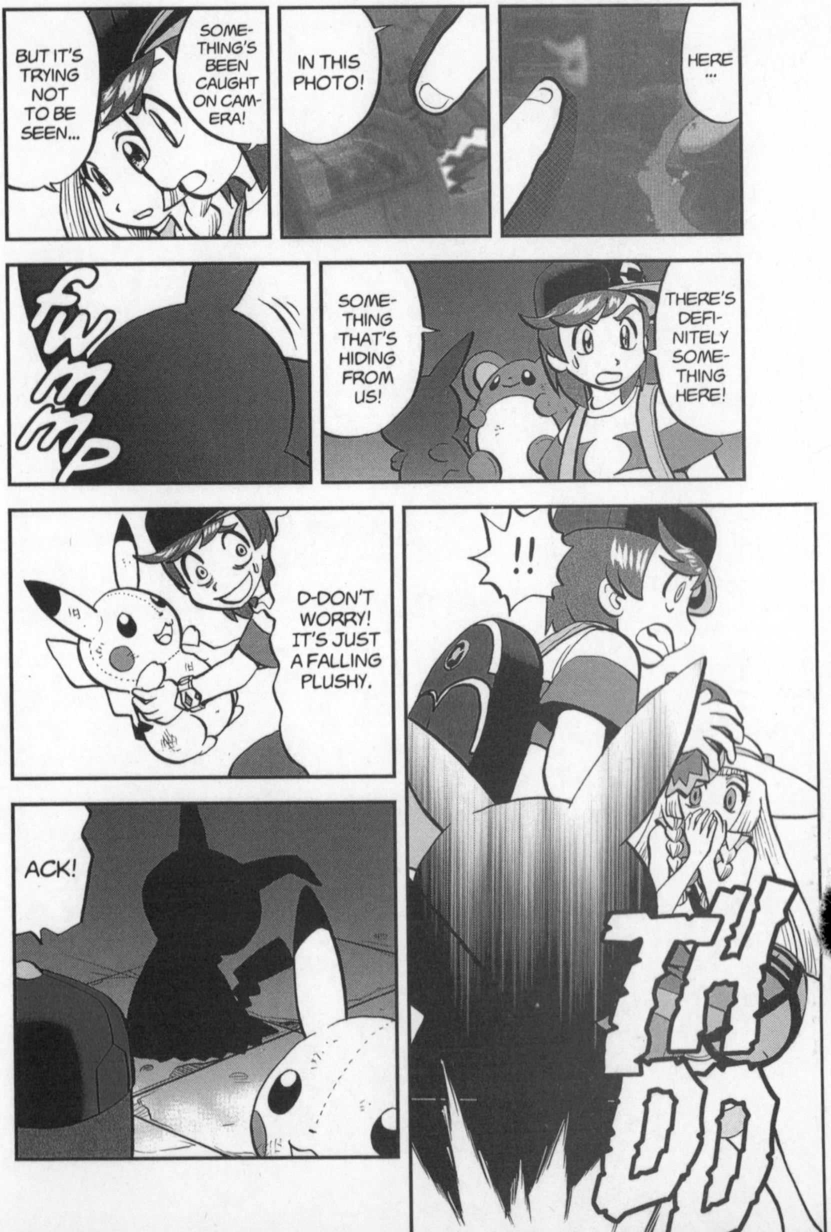
HERE ...
IN THIS PHOTO!
SOME-THING'S BEEN CAUGHT ON CAM-ERA!
BUT IT'S TRYING NOT TO BE SEEN...
THERE'S DEFI-NITELY SOME-THING HERE!
SOME-THING THAT'S HIDING FROM US!
fwmmp
!!
THDD
D-DON'T WORRY! IT'S JUST A FALLING PLUSHY.
ACK!

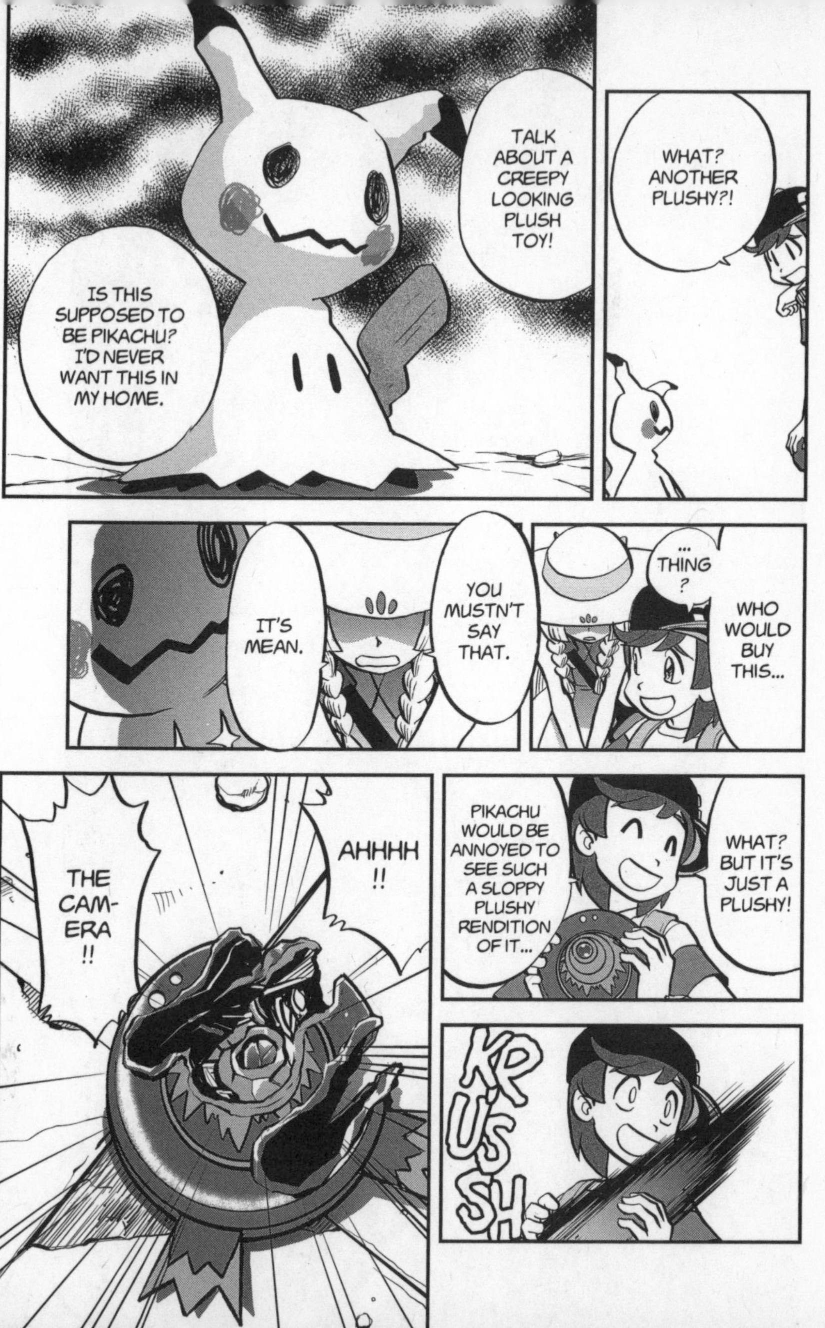
WHAT? ANOTHER PLUSHY?!
TALK ABOUT A CREEPY LOOKING PLUSH TOY!
IS THIS SUPPOSED TO BE PIKACHU? I'D NEVER WANT THIS IN MY HOME.
WHO WOULD BUY THIS...
...THING?
YOU MUSTN'T SAY THAT.
IT'S MEAN.
WHAT? BUT IT'S JUST A PLUSHY!
PIKACHU WOULD BE ANNOYED TO SEE SUCH A SLOPPY PLUSHY RENDITION OF IT...
KRUSSH
AHHHH!!
THE CAM-ERA!!

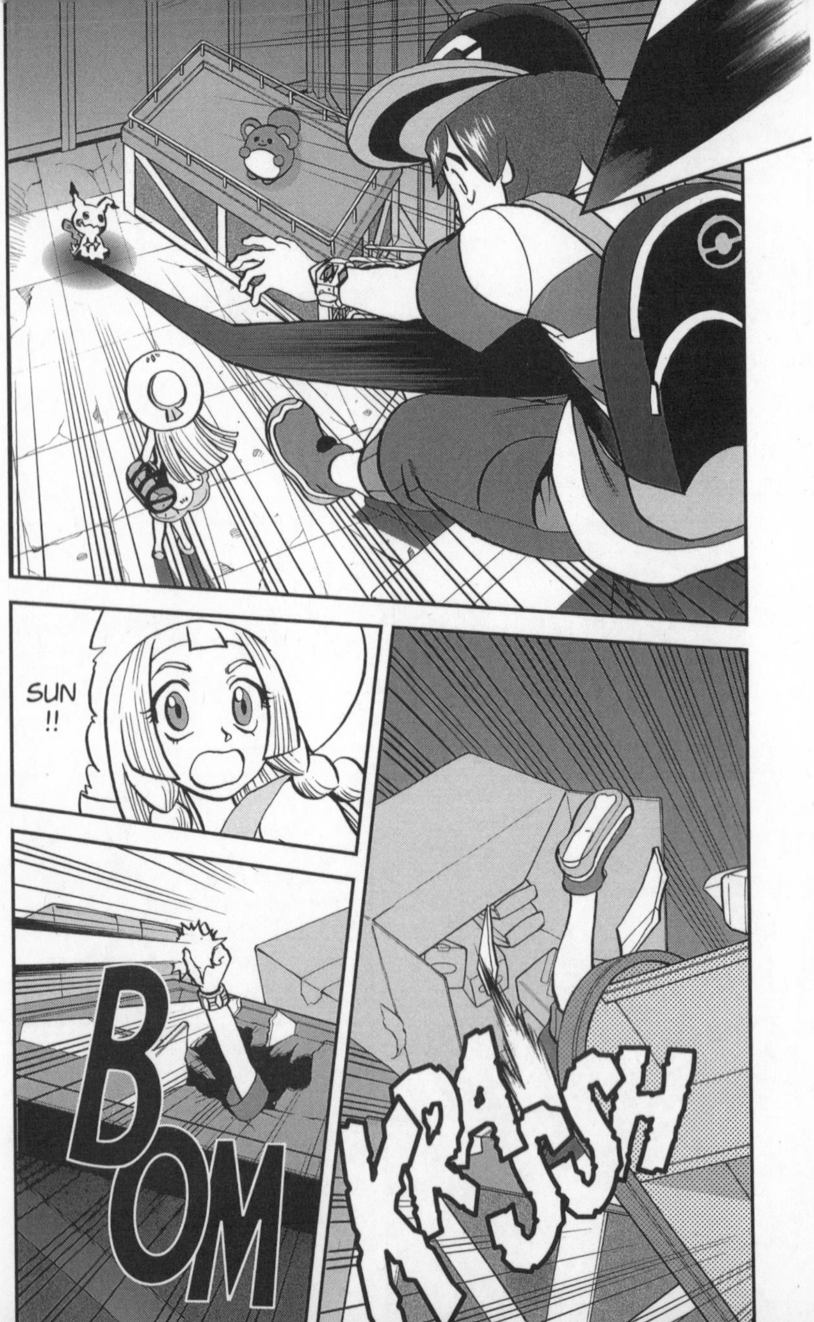
KRASCH
SUN !!
BOOM

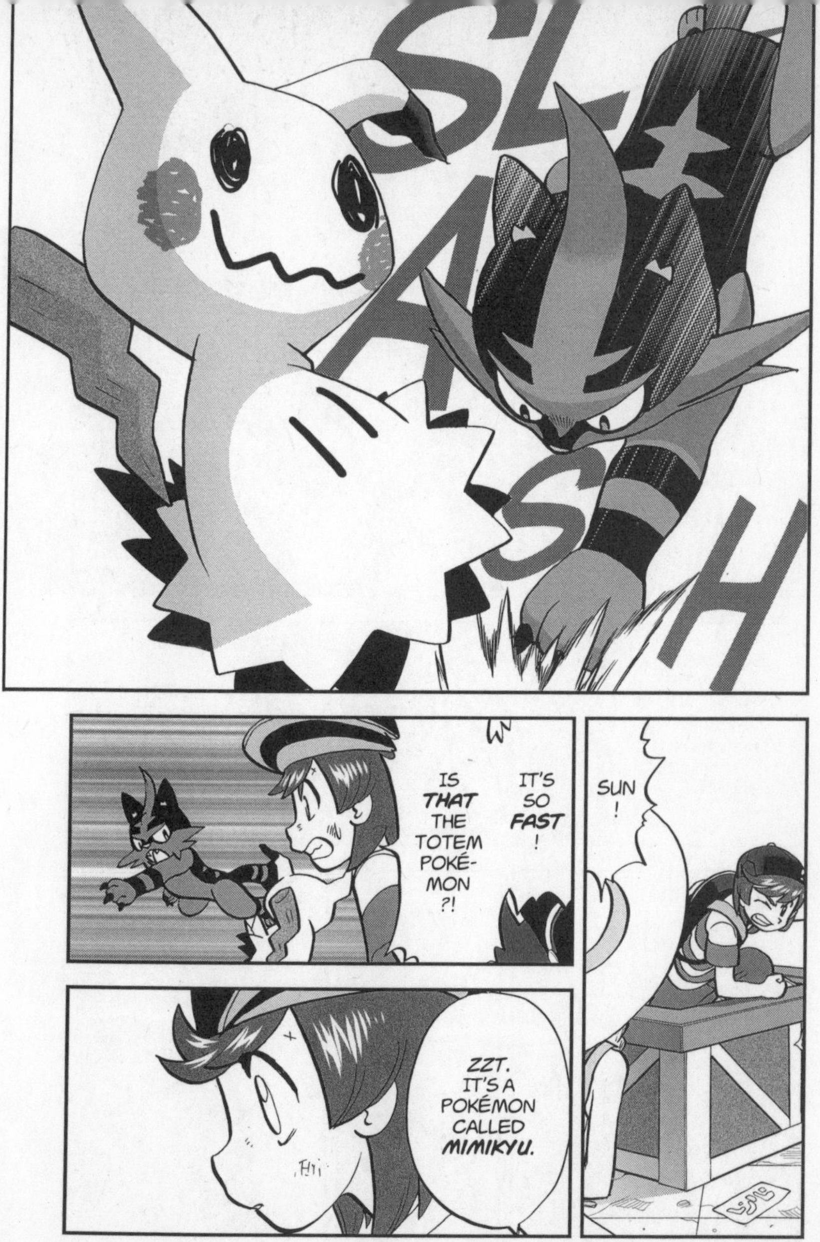
SLASH
SUN!
IT'S SO FAST!
IS THAT THE TOTEM POKÉMON?!
ZZT. IT'S A POKÉMON CALLED MIMIKYU.

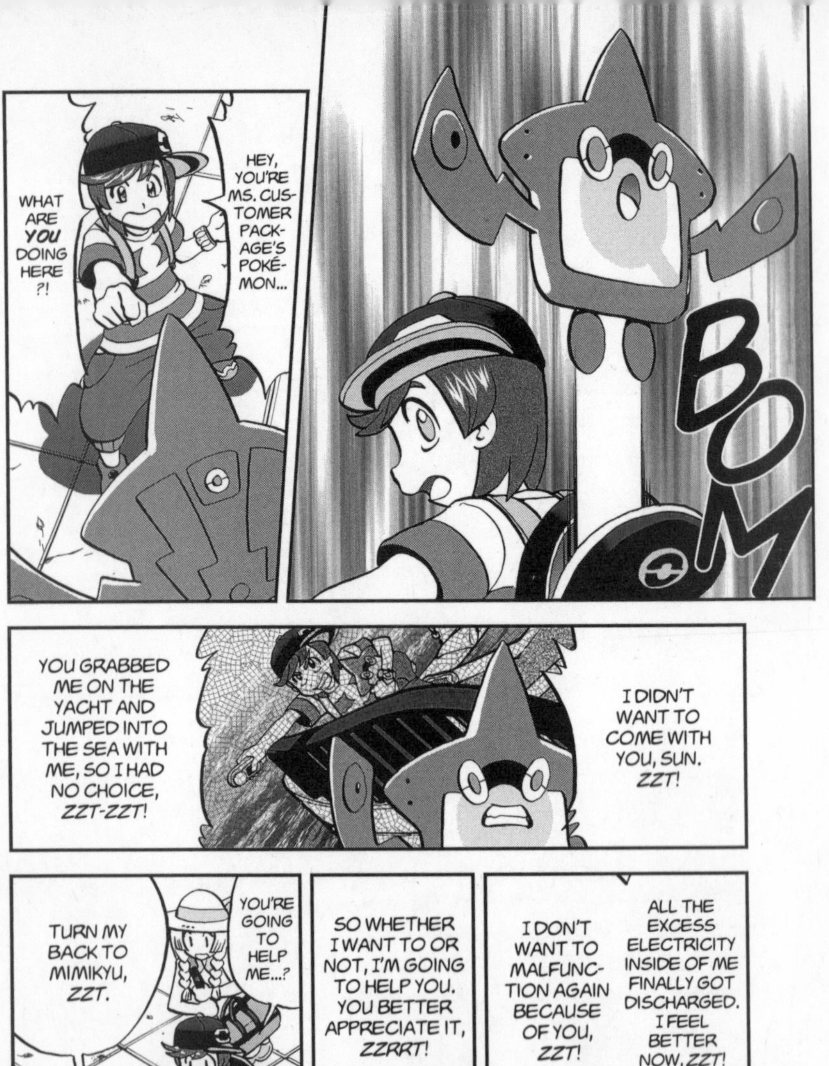
BOM
HEY, YOU'RE MS. CUSTOMER PACKAGE'S POKÉMON...
WHAT ARE **YOU** DOING HERE?!
I DIDN'T WANT TO COME WITH YOU, SUN. *ZZT*!
YOU GRABBED ME ON THE YACHT AND JUMPED INTO THE SEA WITH ME, SO I HAD NO CHOICE, *ZZT-ZZT*!
ALL THE EXCESS ELECTRICITY INSIDE OF ME FINALLY GOT DISCHARGED. I FEEL BETTER NOW, *ZZT*!
I DON'T WANT TO MALFUNCTION AGAIN BECAUSE OF YOU, *ZZT*!
SO WHETHER I WANT TO OR NOT, I'M GOING TO HELP YOU. YOU BETTER APPRECIATE IT, *ZZRRT*!
YOU'RE GOING TO HELP ME...?
TURN MY BACK TO MIMIKYU, *ZZT*.

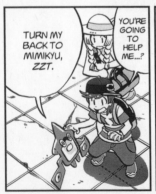

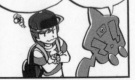

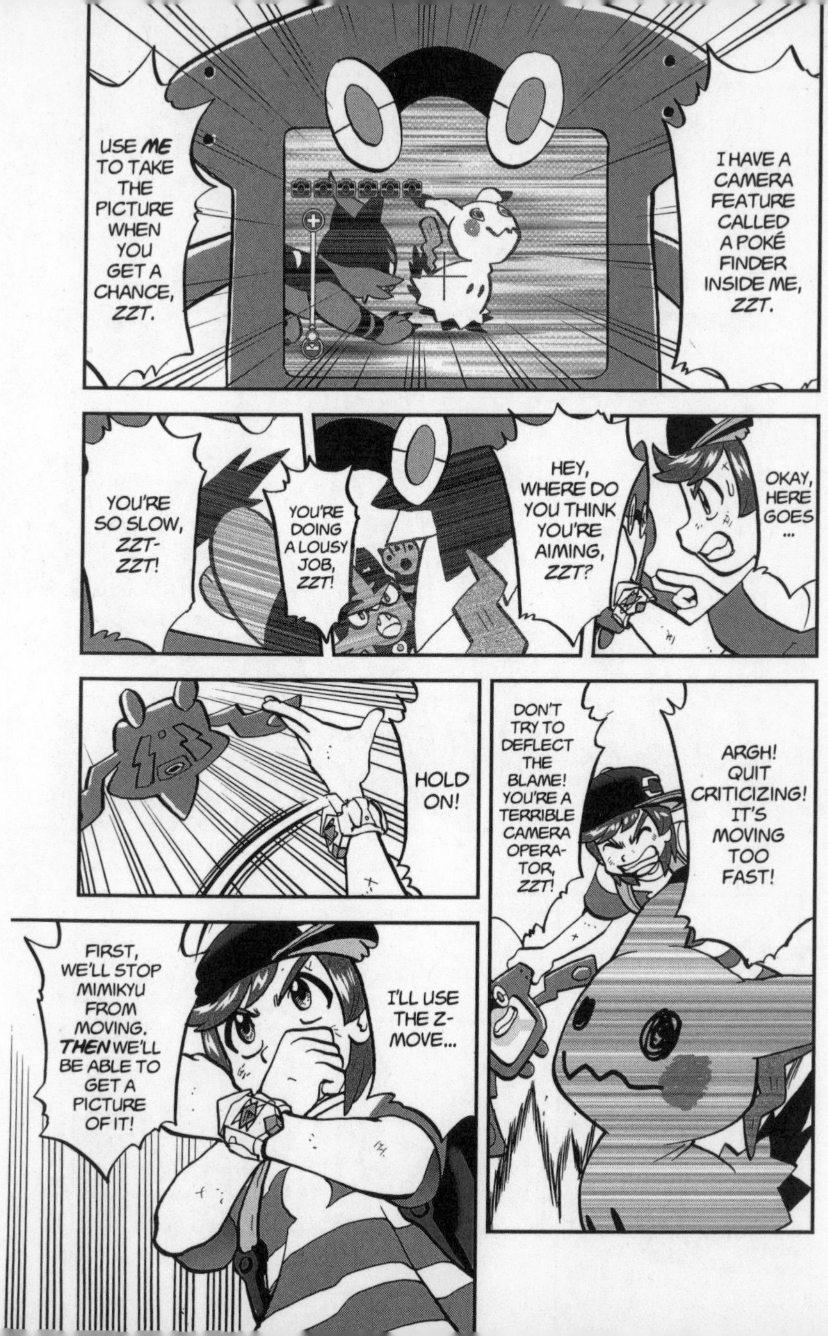
I HAVE A CAMERA FEATURE CALLED A POKÉ FINDER INSIDE ME, ZZT.
USE **ME** TO TAKE THE PICTURE WHEN YOU GET A CHANCE, ZZT.
OKAY, HERE GOES ...
HEY, WHERE DO YOU THINK YOU'RE AIMING, ZZT?
YOU'RE DOING A LOUSY JOB, ZZT!
YOU'RE SO SLOW, ZZT-ZZT!
ARGH! QUIT CRITICIZING! IT'S MOVING TOO FAST!
DON'T TRY TO DEFLECT THE BLAME! YOU'RE A TERRIBLE CAMERA OPERATOR, ZZT!
HOLD ON!
I'LL USE THE Z-MOVE...
FIRST, WE'LL STOP MIMIKYU FROM MOVING. **THEN** WE'LL BE ABLE TO GET A PICTURE OF IT!

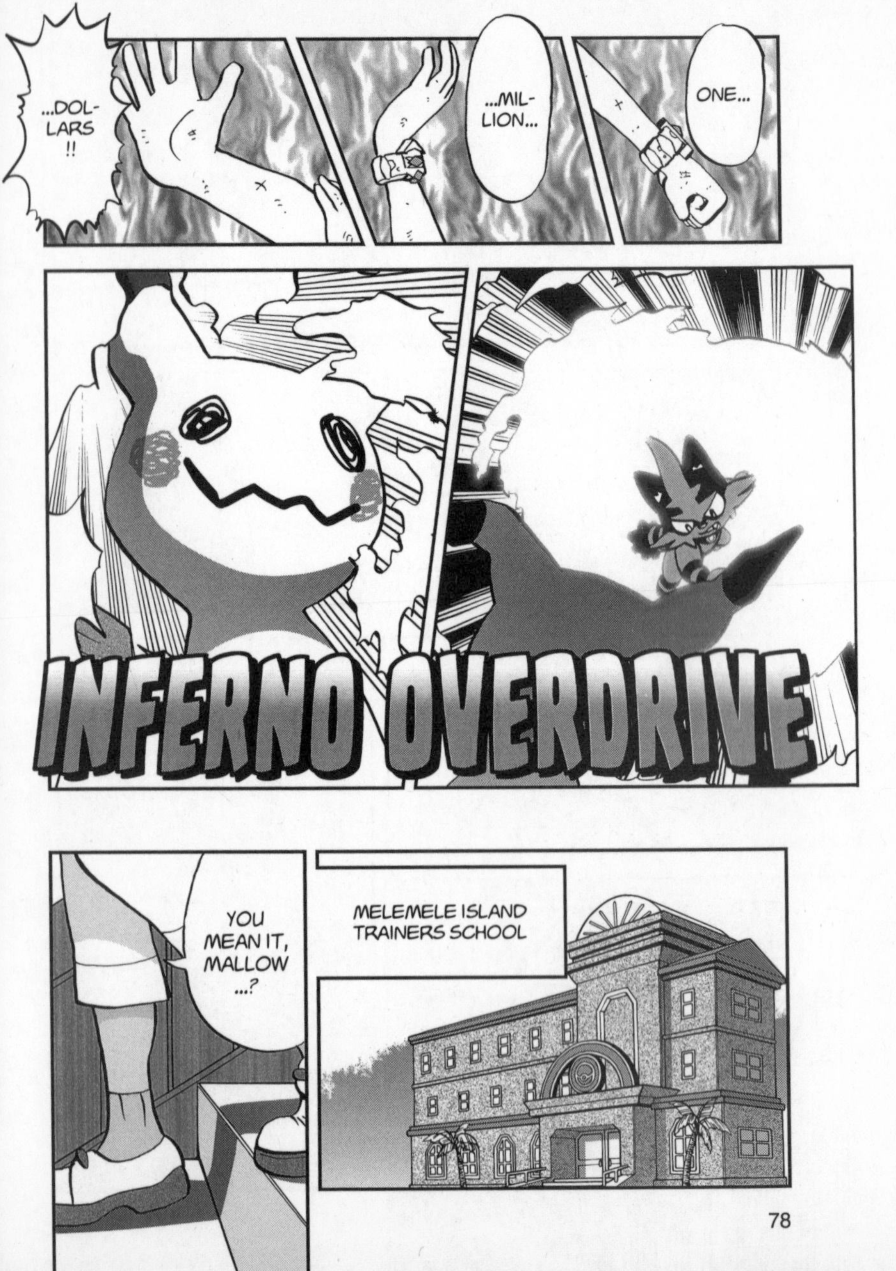
ONE...
...MIL-LION...
...DOL-LARS !!
INFERNO OVERDRIVE
MELEMELE ISLAND TRAINERS SCHOOL
YOU MEAN IT, MALLOW ...?

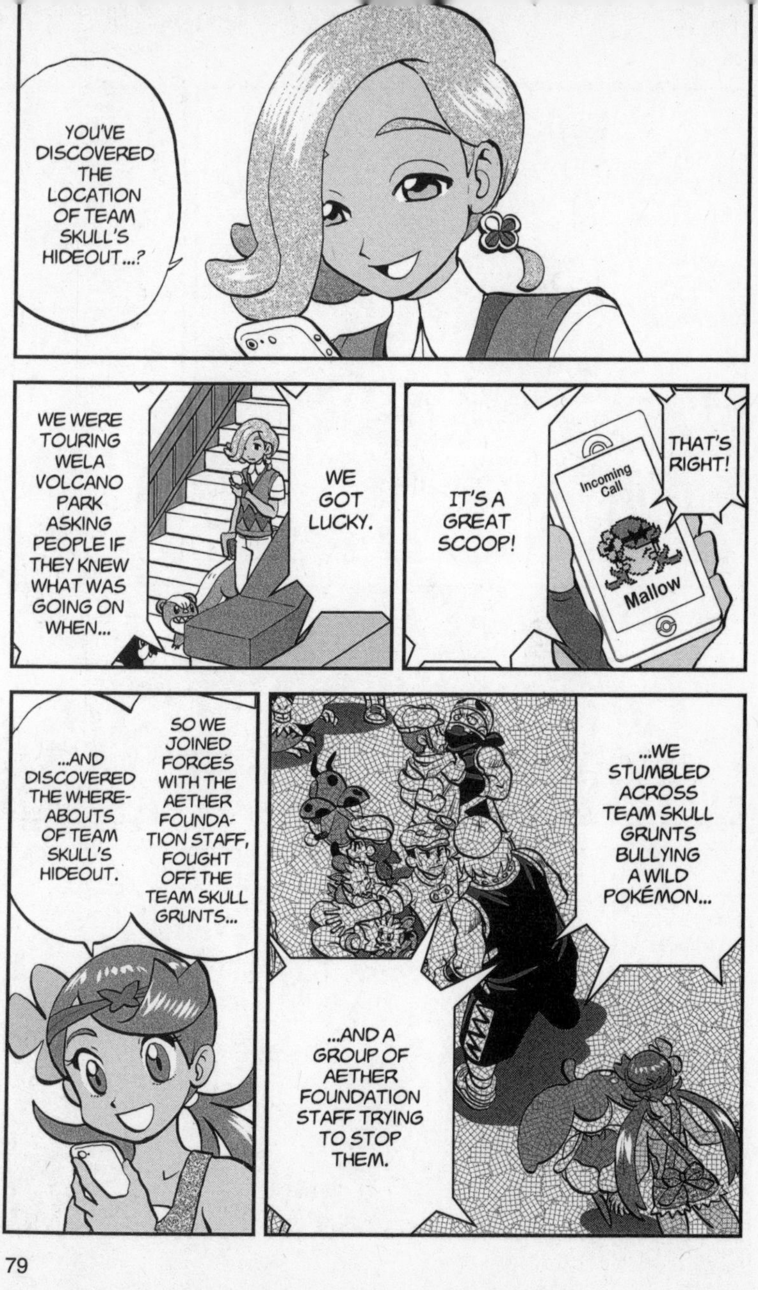
YOU'VE DISCOVERED THE LOCATION OF TEAM SKULL'S HIDEOUT...?
Incoming Call
Mallow
THAT'S RIGHT!
IT'S A GREAT SCOOP!
WE GOT LUCKY.
WE WERE TOURING WELA VOLCANO PARK ASKING PEOPLE IF THEY KNEW WHAT WAS GOING ON WHEN...
...WE STUMBLED ACROSS TEAM SKULL GRUNTS BULLYING A WILD POKÉMON...
...AND A GROUP OF AETHER FOUNDATION STAFF TRYING TO STOP THEM.
SO WE JOINED FORCES WITH THE AETHER FOUNDATION STAFF, FOUGHT OFF THE TEAM SKULL GRUNTS...
...AND DISCOVERED THE WHERE-ABOUTS OF TEAM SKULL'S HIDEOUT.

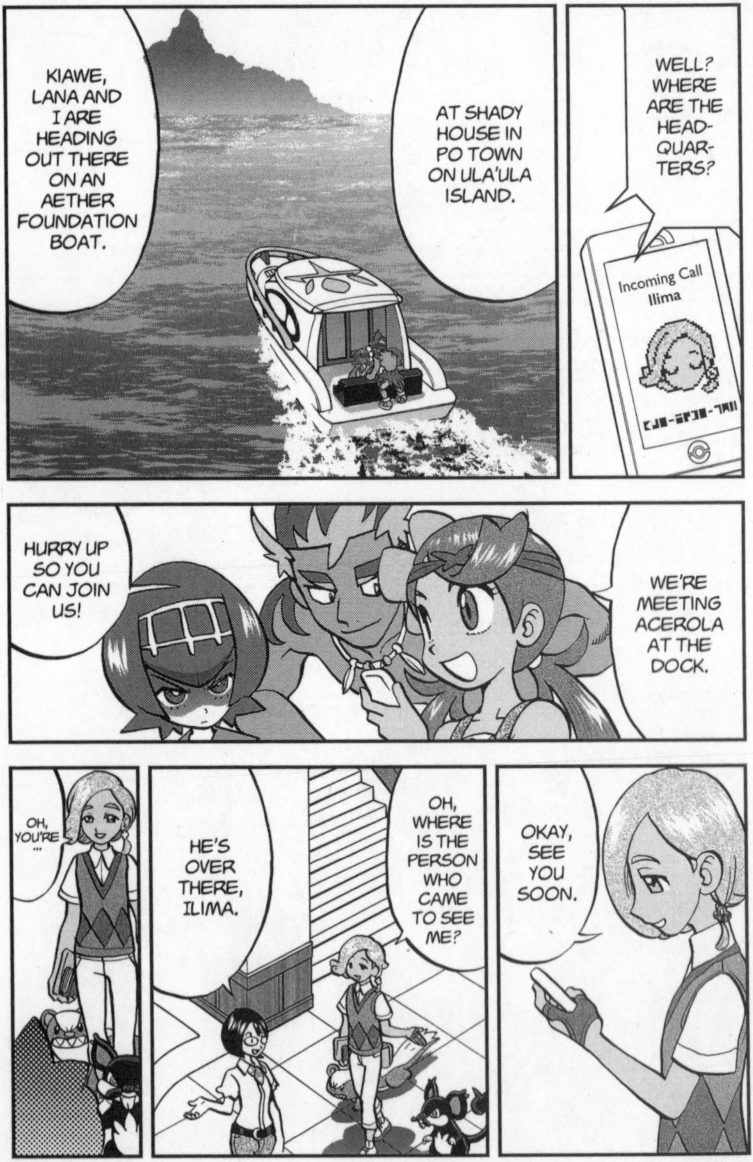
WELL? WHERE ARE THE HEAD-QUAR-TERS?
Incoming Call
Ilima
AT SHADY HOUSE IN PO TOWN ON ULA'ULA ISLAND.
KIAWE, LANA AND I ARE HEADING OUT THERE ON AN AETHER FOUNDATION BOAT.
WE'RE MEETING ACEROLA AT THE DOCK.
HURRY UP SO YOU CAN JOIN US!
OKAY, SEE YOU SOON.
OH, WHERE IS THE PERSON WHO CAME TO SEE ME?
HE'S OVER THERE, ILIMA.
OH, YOU'RE ...

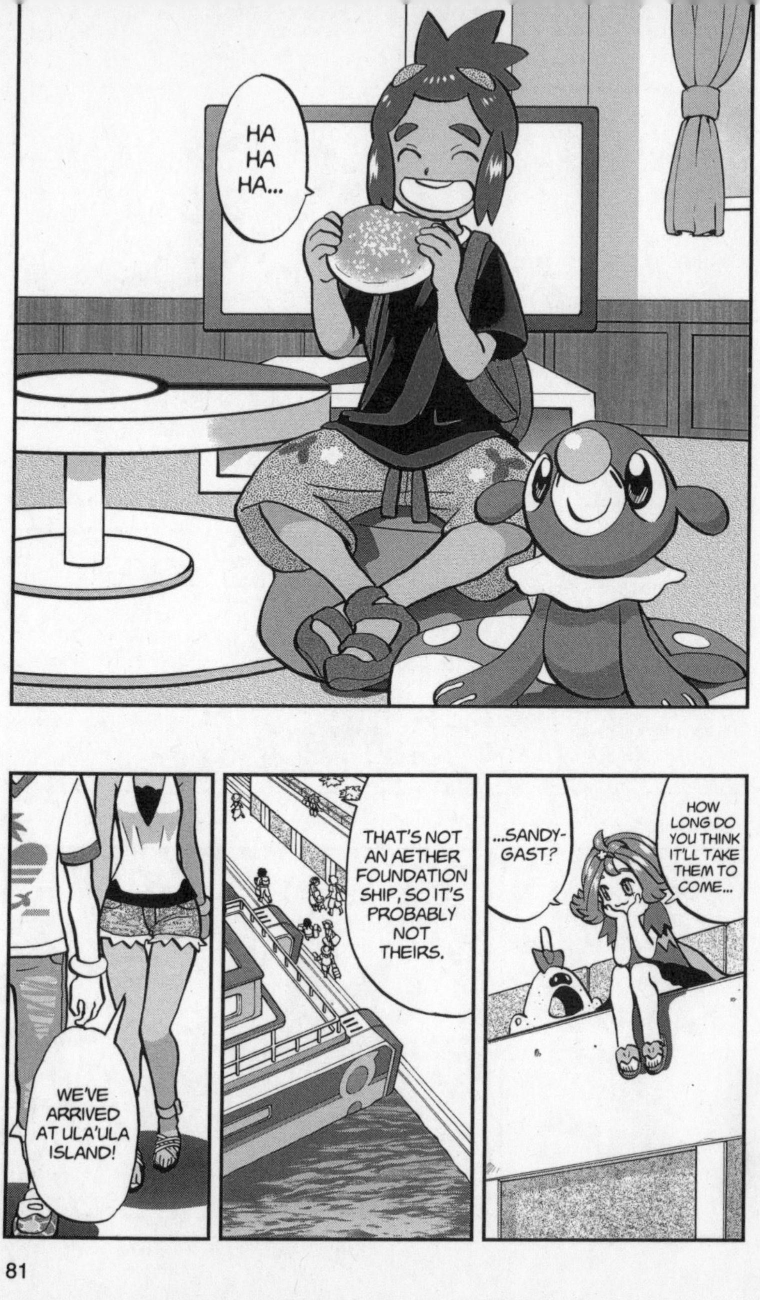
HA HA HA...
HOW LONG DO YOU THINK IT'LL TAKE THEM TO COME...
...SANDY-GAST?
THAT'S NOT AN AETHER FOUNDATION SHIP, SO IT'S PROBABLY NOT THEIRS.
WE'VE ARRIVED AT ULA'ULA ISLAND!

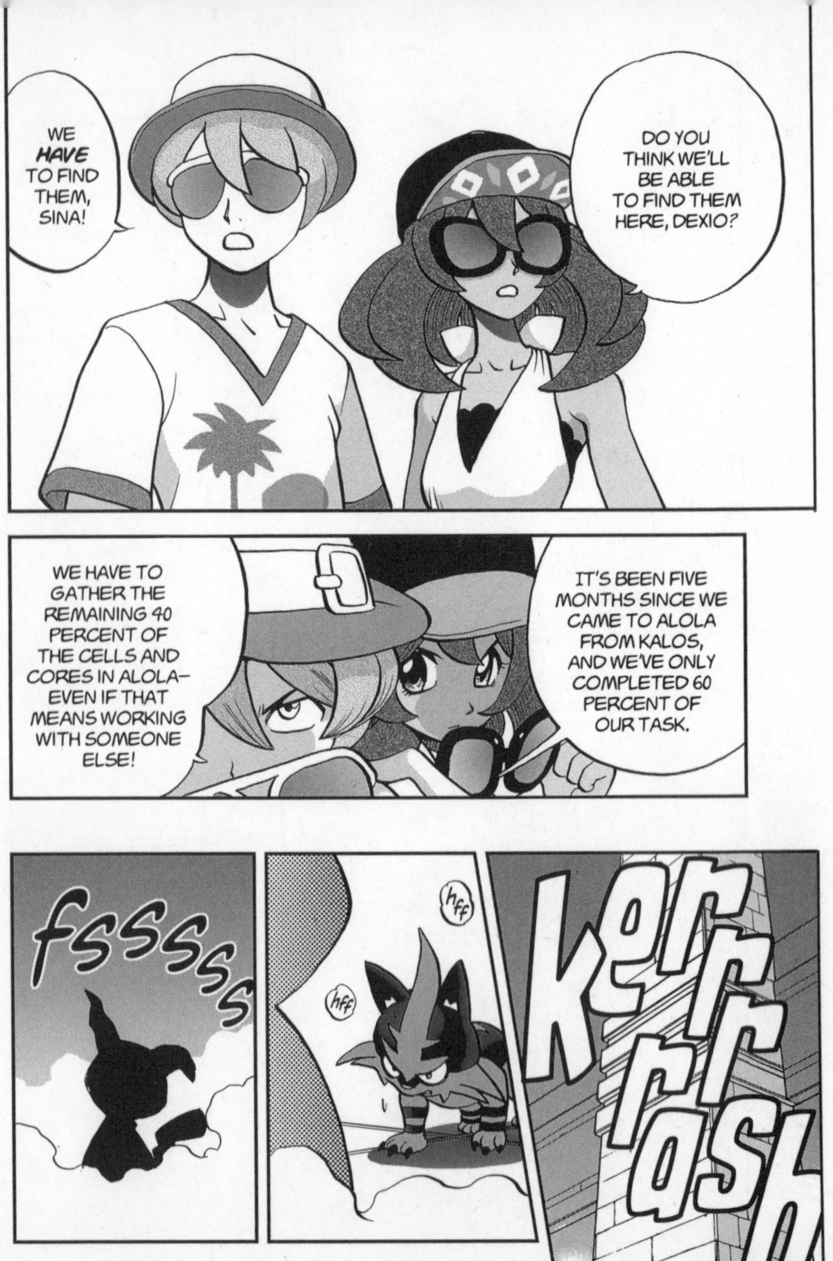

DO YOU THINK WE'LL BE ABLE TO FIND THEM HERE, DEXIO?
WE **HAVE** TO FIND THEM, SINA!
IT'S BEEN FIVE MONTHS SINCE WE CAME TO ALOLA FROM KALOS, AND WE'VE ONLY COMPLETED 60 PERCENT OF OUR TASK.
WE HAVE TO GATHER THE REMAINING 40 PERCENT OF THE CELLS AND CORES IN ALOLA—EVEN IF THAT MEANS WORKING WITH SOMEONE ELSE!
kerrrrrash
hff
hff
fssssss

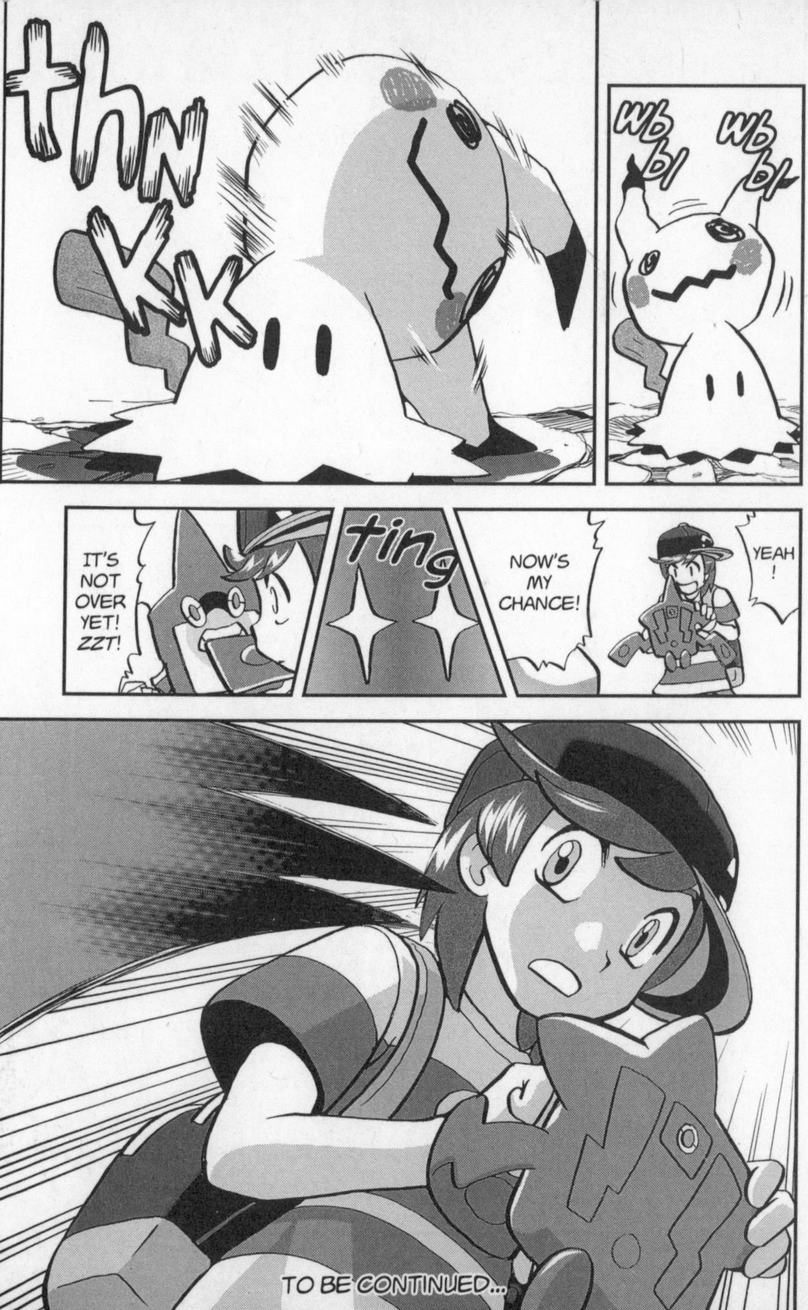

wbbl
wbbl
thnkk
YEAH!
NOW'S MY CHANCE!
ting
IT'S NOT OVER YET! ZZT!
TO BE CONTINUED...

Totem

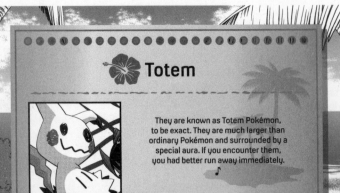

They are known as Totem Pokémon, to be exact. They are much larger than ordinary Pokémon and surrounded by a special aura. If you encounter them, you had better run away immediately.

Guide to Alola 14

**Pokémon Sun & Moon
Volume 5
VIZ Media Edition**

Story by HIDENORI KUSAKA
Art by SATOSHI YAMAMOTO

Original Cover Design—Hiroyuki KAWASOME (grafio)

English Adaptation—Bryant Turnage
Translation—Tetsuichiro Miyaki
Touch-Up & Lettering—Susan Daigle-Leach
Design—Alice Lewis
Editor—Annette Roman

Printed in the U.S.A.

Published by
VIZ Media, LLC
P.O. Box 77010
San Francisco, CA 94107

10 9 8 7 6 5 4 3 2 1
First printing, September 2019

viz.com

Coming Next Volume

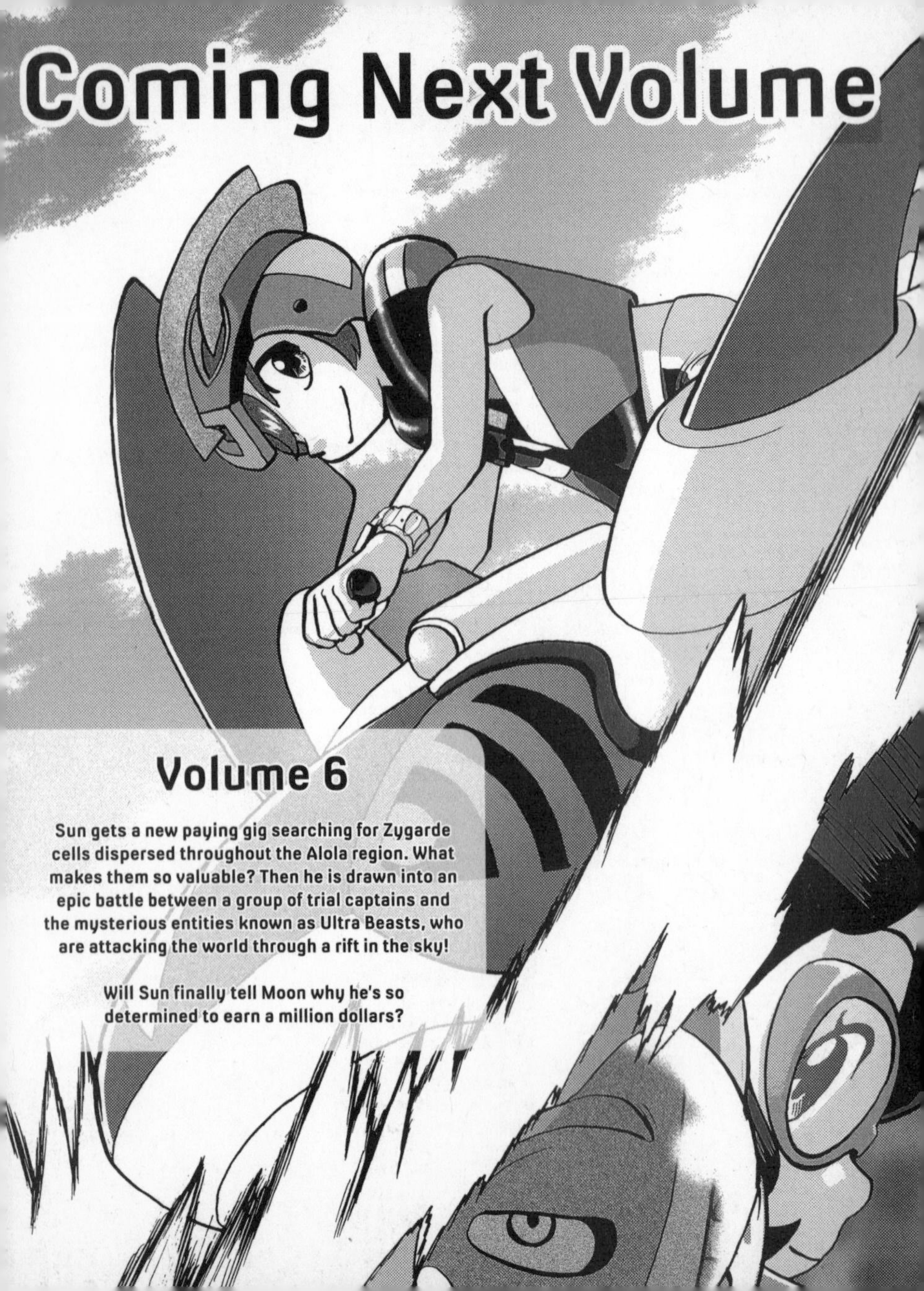

Volume 6

Sun gets a new paying gig searching for Zygarde cells dispersed throughout the Alola region. What makes them so valuable? Then he is drawn into an epic battle between a group of trial captains and the mysterious entities known as Ultra Beasts, who are attacking the world through a rift in the sky!

Will Sun finally tell Moon why he's so determined to earn a million dollars?

THE ART OF

STORY AND ART BY
Satoshi Yamamoto

A collection of beautiful full-color art from the artist of the Pokémon Adventures graphic novel series! In addition to illustrations of your favorite Pokémon, this vibrant volume includes exclusive sketches and storyboards, four pull-out posters, and an exclusive manga side story!

viz.com

THIS IS THE END OF THIS GRAPHIC NOVEL!

To properly enjoy this VIZ Media graphic novel, please turn it around and begin reading from right to left.

This book has been printed in the original Japanese format in order to preserve the orientation of the original artwork. Have fun with it!

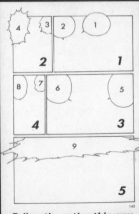

Follow the action this way.

≪≪≪ READ THIS WAY!